RNWMP: BRIDE FOR ELIJAH

MAIL ORDER MOUNTIES

KAY P. DAWSON

To sign up for newsletter alerts, TEXT 'DAWSON' to 42828

INTRODUCTION

Mail Order Mounties is a multi-author series set in Canada during the early 1900's. Join authors Kirsten Osbourne, Kay P. Dawson, Cassie Hayes and Amelia Adams as they bring you fictional stories about members of the Royal Northwest Mounted Police, and the mail order brides who love them.

RNWMP: Bride for Elijah is the second book in the Mail Order Mounties Series

What does a wealthy, pampered woman from the city have in common with a simple Mountie on the frontier?

Nothing—and that's exactly why Miss Hazel Hughes decides they need each other.

Rose Lambert has grown up in the wealthy society of Ottawa, but longs for a life where people will respect her for who she is, and not what her family's status can give them. After her fiancé leaves her reputation in tatters, she knows she needs to get away somewhere for a fresh start—somewhere where she will have a say in her own life.

Elijah Thorpe didn't think he needed a wife, believing it wouldn't be fair for a woman to marry a Mountie, only to be left a widow if something happened. But when Miss Hazel Hughes decides a man should be married, he soon finds out that she will get her way. Before he knows it, he has a woman on her way out to to British Columbia to become his bride.

When they meet, he soon realizes the woman he's been bound to isn't quite what he'd expected.

What will happen when two strangers are brought together, unsure of their decision to marry? And when the past catches up and threatens to destroy the shaky foundation they've started to build, can their love withstand the forces trying to keep them apart?

CHAPTER 1

"Get your hands off me, you filthy swine." Rose pulled her hand back and was already bringing the palm of it across his cheek as the door opened. The loud gasp that reached her ears drowned out the crack of her hand on the man's skin. Slowly turning her head, she knew the moment she saw her mother and the other woman standing there, they weren't going to believe anything she had to say.

They'd already made up their minds.

She was in the arms of Robert Harvey, with the front of her dress torn just enough to expose the white of her skin underneath. It wouldn't matter if she tried to say she'd been fighting him off, because everyone knew Robert was the man who'd been chosen for her to marry. He was one of the most sought-after bachelors in all of Ottawa. And the man who'd been chosen to partner in her father's law firm.

All this meant was that there would be no way she could get out of marrying him.

While some things had come a long way in the past few decades, a woman's reputation could still be destroyed in one instance. She could then be forced to marry the man who she'd been caught alone with in the society she lived in—the wealthy elite of Ottawa.

Well, she wasn't going to end up stuck being married to a man she despised, no matter what damage her reputation suffered.

"Mother. Mrs. Franks." Nodding to the women, she tried to walk by them with her head held high, while pulling her blouse back over to cover herself. As she got beside them, her skirt got caught on a metal vase sitting near the doorway, and the entire pot overturned with a loud crash.

She stopped and tightly clenched her eyes briefly, not even wanting to turn around to see the damage she'd just done. Of course she wouldn't be able to make an exit with her dignity intact.

Taking a deep breath, she continued walking, never looking back. She'd rather be sent through the gates of hell, forced to sit with the devil himself, than to end up married to Robert Harvey. So, with the sound of the vase still rolling and echoing loudly across the room, she made her feet take one step in front of the other as she kept going out the door.

No, this time, she was going to take matters into her own hands. She wasn't sure how yet, but she knew she was going to have to leave the sheltered existence she'd lived in Ottawa behind.

And she realized with a start, she'd never been more excited in her life.

~

SHE HATED LYING, but she didn't see any other way around it. Her plan was already in motion, and by the time anyone realized what she'd done, it would be too late to do anything about it.

"I'm sure going to miss you, Rose."

Rose set her bag down and went over to put her arms around her friend. Claire Anderson was a maid who worked at their house, but Rose had never thought of her as anything less than a friend. She'd been her confidante, and often the only one to show her any compassion or kindness while Rose's parents worked so hard to rise in the ranks of Ottawa society.

The girls often snuck away together to talk to each other about their dreams and what they hoped for their future. Claire was a hopeless romantic, and she believed in true love. Rose wanted to believe in that too, but from what she'd seen in her own parent's marriage, she wasn't sure it was real.

"I know, Claire. I wish you could come with me. I promise to write, and maybe someday, you can come out there to see me." Rose tried to keep her lip from trembling as she pulled back and looked into her friend's tear-filled eyes.

She knew it was unlikely that Claire could ever afford to travel out west. And Rose doubted she'd ever be welcomed back here in Ottawa once her parents found out what she'd done. So truthfully, they both knew it was probably the last time they would see each other.

"What is he like? Did Miss Hazel tell you much about him? Is he handsome?"

Rose smiled as Claire asked the very questions she'd known her friend would ask. It was the first time they'd really had a chance to sit and talk alone since Miss Hazel Hughes had approached Rose at church on Sunday. She would be heading to begin her training in just a few days, so she had been secretly trying to pack more of her belongings than anyone knew.

Her parents believed she was being trained in the wifely duties for her marriage to Robert. They couldn't understand why she was insisting on the training since Robert would be a partner in her father's law firm, and they would have maids as she was accustomed to.

Rose had insisted she wanted to be the best wife possible. She wanted to go to Miss Hazel's to learn everything she could before getting married.

Claire was the only one who knew the truth.

She had no intentions of marrying Robert, and would be leaving on a train headed to British Columbia on the first of October. And when she arrived, Rose would be marrying a stranger.

A Mountie who Miss Hazel Hughes had met, and who she'd decided needed a wife.

"I don't know any more than I've already told you. Miss Hazel says that Elijah is a kind and quiet man, and he needs someone who can bring out the laughter in him. And most importantly, he will protect me if I need it."

Claire wrinkled her eyes together like she always did when she was annoyed. "Robert Harvey better not even think of chasing you out there. If he does, I hope your Mountie takes care of him and lets him know that you're no longer someone he can try bending to his will."

Rose rolled her eyes. "He's not *my Mountie*, Claire." Although she had to admit to feeling a certain tingle in her stomach as she said the words. She knew it was crazy to be running across the country to marry a stranger, but somehow she sensed that this man Elijah would treat her better than the man she'd be forced to marry if she stayed here.

This way, she could have some control of her own life, and get away from the stifling life she led under her parent's watchful eyes.

"I still can't believe Hazel Hughes just came right up to you and said she thought you'd be perfect as a Mountie's wife where her son was working. Or that you'd be so quick to agree for that matter!"

"Trust me, when Miss Hazel has an idea, she doesn't back down easily. I knew the minute she came over to me she had something in mind. I've spoken to her quite a few times over the years at church, so I could tell this time, she wasn't just coming to make small talk."

Rose was leaning into her wardrobe, carefully

choosing which dresses she would take with her as she talked with Claire. She hadn't realized quite how far she had her head inside until a loud clap startled her, making her bang her head on the corner of a small wardrobe shelf.

As Claire's voice followed, saying how romantic it all sounded, Rose had difficulty hearing through the ringing in her ears. She reached up to rub the spot that had been wounded as she quickly spun around to glare at her friend.

"Claire, look what you made me do! I just hit my head so hard I'm seeing stars. Get the notion out of your own head that this is some kind of romantic trip I'm going on."

Claire just laughed. "Rose, you and I both know you'd have likely banged your head regardless of what I was doing." She clapped her hands again for emphasis. "And, I have a feeling you might be in for more than you even realize when you head out to marry your Mountie."

Rose just kept massaging the bump that was already forming and shook her head in Claire's direction.

"I've told you already, he's not *my Mountie*!"

CHAPTER 2

"*A*ll right ladies, you want to make sure you use a sharp knife to cut the chicken into pieces. First, you will want to pull open the thigh and gently cut it from the body. Then, you can chop off the legs." Miss Hazel slammed the knife down, viciously slicing off the first leg of the chicken.

Rose's hand flew to cover her mouth as a loud gasp escaped. She started to back away from the side cupboard where the raw chicken was now lying with only one leg sticking in the air. However, with another sharp swing of her arm, Miss Hazel quickly removed that one too and tossed it into some flour, then into the bowl of batter they'd just finished mixing up.

"Now, you will continue cutting the chicken

pieces, making sure to use up all of the meat on the bird."

Her eyes widened as Miss Hazel continued to hack at the poor dead animal on the counter. She kept cutting and removing pieces of the flesh, then flipping them into the batter.

Rose had been feeling so proud of herself as they had worked at mixing up the batter for the fried chicken. Miss Hazel had said it would be something the men out west would love, and it would be a staple food they could make for their husbands. Along with the meat from the chicken, she was then going to show them how to use the bones and left overs to make a delicious chicken soup.

Rose had managed to measure out the ingredients and had been feeling quite confident in her ability to learn to cook.

Until Miss Hazel had flopped the carcass of a dead bird on the counter in front of her.

And things had been rapidly sliding downhill ever since.

She continued backing up, holding her hand over her mouth for fear a scream would escape if she brought it down. Suddenly, her backside made contact with something and before she could turn to see what it was, a loud crash broke through the room.

As she jumped and spun around, she watched in horror as the pans filled with the ingredients they'd set out to make the soup clattered to the floor. They had placed everything on the table ready to use while the fried chicken cooked, and now everything was falling to the ground like a waterfall.

Horrified, Rose knelt down and started picking some of the ingredients up while the echoes of the pans still vibrated through the room. "Oh, I'm so sorry. I didn't mean to..." Her voice cracked as she struggled to keep back the tears.

She realized another girl had joined her, so she slowly lifted her eyes, afraid of what she would see on her face. It was Tilly, the one who seemed to be able to do all of these tasks with ease. Tilly smiled at her, before putting her head back down to help with the clean-up.

These girls must all think she was completely hopeless. And truthfully, when it came to any household duties, she was.

She'd never had to do anything like this before. She'd certainly never thought about where her chicken pieces would have come from.

These girls would make good wives for all of

their Mounties. Her poor Mountie would likely end up with food poisoning and die of hypothermia when she couldn't even wash his clothing for him.

Standing up tall, she tried not to let herself look at the others. She faced Miss Hazel, who was still standing and watching her in shock with the knife held in the air. "If you'll excuse me, Miss Hazel, I'm not feeling well."

She didn't even wait for permission to leave. Turning quickly on her heel, she walked from the room as fast as she could go. And as she did, she sent a silent prayer of forgiveness up to all the chickens she'd ever eaten in her lifetime.

∾

ROSE STOOD LOOKING out the window to the street below. As she watched the people milling around, she wrung her hands together, swallowing hard to keep the lump in her throat from choking her.

Why did she ever think she could do this?

She'd grown up with maids and cooks and helpers for everything she wanted. Anything she needed was done for her.

And she'd honestly thought she could learn enough to move out to the untamed west and be a good wife to some poor man who deserved far better than she could ever give.

But what other options did she have? She'd grown to hate the life she was living in Ottawa. The fact that she was waited on by everyone around her was starting to make her feel useless. She wanted to be able to care for herself, and do simple tasks like cook a meal for someone.

She wanted more for her life, including a home and a family of her own. And a man who could possibly love her for herself, and not for the wealth her family had.

A gentle knock sounded at the door, and she reached up to wipe at her eyes. She couldn't let anyone see the tears that had been threatening to spill over. Since she'd lied and said she wasn't feeling well, she quickly went over and sat on the bed, not wanting them to catch her standing and looking out the window. It hadn't been completely a lie anyway. After seeing that poor chicken on the counter, she really hadn't been feeling very good.

"Come in." She cupped her hands tightly together on her knees.

When the door opened, Miss Hazel peeked her head around and smiled at her. "I hope I'm not disturbing you. You looked quite distraught when you left."

The older woman came into the room, softly shutting the door behind her before walking over and sitting next to Rose on the edge of the bed.

"You know, we all have to start somewhere when we learn new things. You don't need to feel embarrassed that you can't do some of these tasks I'm teaching you girls."

Rose couldn't even lift her eyes to look at Hazel. But she could sense the woman's eyes were intently watching her.

"I don't know even the simplest of tasks. I want to learn, but how can I when I can't even cope with seeing a dead chicken lying in front of me? I've eaten chicken all my life, but never once had to see how it had looked before it ended up on my plate."

She kept her head down, waiting for Miss Hazel to speak. Surely she would tell Rose she wouldn't be a good choice to go out and marry a man who would need a competent wife to look after him.

Miss Hazel reached out and placed her hand over hers. "Rose dear, I've known you for many years now. I've watched you grow up, coming to church every Sunday with your family. And I've seen the kind of woman you've grown into. I can see who you are, even if you can't see it yourself yet. That's why I chose you for Elijah. I knew you'd be a perfect fit for him."

Elijah. Every time she heard his name, her heart would skip a beat. She couldn't understand why, but there was just something about his name that made her feel hope in her chest.

She finally lifted her head and looked at Miss Hazel. "But why? Surely you must know other women who'd be better suited. Women who can cook for him, and wash his clothes, and keep his home clean. I'll be lucky if I don't end up burning his house down around him."

Miss Hazel chuckled softly and shook her head. "Maybe. But I also think he needs someone just like you. Someone who can make him smile and make him happy."

Rose wrinkled her eyebrows together. "Do you really think I can make him happy? Even if I can't do the basic tasks a wife should know how to do?"

Hazel patted her hands, then stood up. "By the time I'm done with you, you'll be able to hold your own in the kitchen. Tilly has also offered to give you some help, if you'll let her."

As she walked to the door, Hazel stopped and

turned back to smile at her. "And, dear, I have no doubt you can make Elijah happy."

Rose watched her leave, then sat staring at the closed door. If Miss Hazel believed she could do it, then Rose knew she had to keep trying.

She just hoped Elijah was a patient man.

CHAPTER 3

*E*lijah Thorpe had never really been known for being patient. It irritated him that they'd had no luck finding the thief who'd stolen from the mercantile, even after chasing him all day. He seemed to have vanished into thin air. And now, as he rode along the trail with his fellow Mounties, his thoughts started to wander to the woman he was supposed to be marrying when he got back to town tomorrow.

How had he ever let himself agree to this? The more he thought about it, the more he started to question his own sanity.

Miss Hazel could be very persuasive, though. And she'd decided the Mounties who worked with her son Theodore needed to be married. The next thing he knew, he was waiting for a woman to arrive and become his wife. A woman he'd never met.

He had to admit in getting a bit caught up in the excitement of Theodore and Jess falling in love and getting married. He was thoroughly enjoying having someone cook delicious meals for them every day. The thought of having his own wife to do that for him was the one thing that helped him believe it might not be such a bad idea to go through with this crazy plan of Miss Hazel's.

Nolan and Kendall rode ahead, talking about their own future brides. He preferred to stay back a bit and not join in the conversation. He didn't even know what he was feeling, so making idle chatter with the other men seemed pointless to him.

They'd been tracking the mercantile outlaw for a few hours already, and he knew the women would be arriving any time now. He wished he could have been there to meet the train and see her for himself to be sure he was doing the right thing. He hoped when he saw her for the first time, he'd have some kind of feeling that would tell him she was going to be suitable.

His eyes scanned the land around him as he tried to imagine a woman coming from the city to live in the wilderness of British Columbia. He wasn't sure of many details about the woman who was coming here to marry him, but he hoped she was capable and had experience she could bring with her to help her adjust.

The mountains loomed in the distance, casting a shadow on the grassy land around them as the horses picked their way along the path. There were so many places for the outlaw to lose the men who were trailing him, so they needed to keep their wits about them as they continued their search.

But the way the other men were going on about the brides they hadn't met yet, had him believing the outlaw could walk right out in front of them and not be noticed.

He reached up to push at the curl that always managed to work its way out from under his hat, no matter how hard he tried to keep it tucked away. He'd heard on more than one occasion to just cut it off, but it wasn't something he was able to do. That curl was something he always remembered his grandma telling him how special it made him when he'd complain about it as a young boy.

He'd been a quiet boy who would rather read a book than play baseball, so he sometimes imagined that curl hanging down was the only thing that made him different.

He knew how silly it was now, but he still wasn't prepared to get rid of it.

"Are you two going to spend all day swooning over women you've never even met? Or could we try to catch this thief so we can get back and actually meet the women who've come all this way to marry our sorry hides."

Kicking his horse forward, he decided it was time to get this job done so he could meet his future wife.

~

THE SOUND of the whistle blowing as it rounded the corner made her jump. She'd been terribly uncomfortable the whole ride west, and the farther she'd gotten from Ottawa, the more doubts had managed to work their way into her head. She was thankful for the company of the other women, including Miss Hazel.

Now, as the train pulled into the station, Rose could feel every heart beat pounding against her chest. What if she couldn't manage out here? What would her new husband think of her?

So many unanswered questions and worries, and there was no going back. With a hiss, the train stopped and people started to stand up to get off. Frantically, her eyes moved around the car, and Miss Hazel smiled at her as she stood. The woman came and patted her hand.

"Have confidence in yourself. I wouldn't have chosen you as a bride for Elijah if I didn't think you'd make a good wife for him. Just trust me. I'm never wrong." Hazel winked at her as she grabbed her bag from the seat and turned to start shooing the women off the train.

"Come on, girls. You have men waiting for you!"

Smoke filled the air around them as she stepped onto the step and out to the platform. Once she could see past the haze, she couldn't stop the gasp that came from her mouth. Everything around her looked so primitive, but behind the buildings was the most beautiful scenery she'd ever imagined.

There were trees everywhere, and as she slowly turned to take it all in, she finally saw the mountains in the distance. She'd grown up in the city with nothing that resembled anything like what she was seeing here. For a moment, panic began to rise in her chest again.

She vaguely noticed Miss Hazel running to hug

her son, Theodore. Rose remembered him from church, as she did Jess, his new wife. But she didn't see any other men standing there with the rather dashing and handsome red jackets like the one Theodore was wearing.

Had the men had a change of heart?

After days of riding out here, she was tired. All she wanted to do was find somewhere to lie down and rest without the constant motion and noise of the train. If Elijah wasn't here, where was she expected to go?

"Well, it would seem that the men, except for Joel, have been called out on assignment. Jess is taking JoAnn over to Kendall's place, so Theodore has offered to help me get the rest of you to your new homes. Honestly, you'd think men would have more common sense than to disappear when they have women coming to marry them."

Rose had to smile at the way Miss Hazel was tutting and clucking her tongue, obviously seriously annoyed at the lack of welcome the women were receiving, as if frontier men could just pick and choose their assignments. Truthfully, Rose was almost grateful for the chance to freshen up a bit and hopefully get her nerves under control before meeting the man she'd come here to marry.

Theodore was talking to some men about bringing their trunks, so Rose let herself have more time to take in the sights of her new home.

As she marveled at the beauty around her, her eyes stopped at movement just past the edge of the building up the dusty street.

What was that creature with the large horns sticking from his head?

If she didn't know any better, she'd almost swear that animal was shaking his head at her and laughing. She blinked hard, sure she was seeing things. When she looked again, it was sauntering off while people moved out of its way.

"Oh, and be sure to stay away from any wild animals you see around here, especially that nuisance of a moose that is always in town." Theodore walked back over to the women, bending over to pick up a couple of the bags he could carry himself.

"You mean him?" Rose pointed in the direction of the beast walking away from them.

Theodore's eyes followed where she pointed, then rolled as he shook his head. "Yes, that's him. He's always hanging around, and while he might look cute and harmless, you never know with a moose. So make sure you all stay clear of any animals you see."

Rose couldn't take her eyes off the animal. If that's what people around here considered cute and harmless, she'd be terrified to meet the ones they considered beastly and dangerous.

CHAPTER 4

"Surely you aren't serious?" Rose's voice was barely more than a whisper as she slowly moved her head to take in the shack she had just walked into. She swallowed hard to keep the scream from making its way out of her own throat. "I knew things would be more primitive out here than back home, but I'd expected it to be just a bit more civilized."

The other girls were waiting outside to be taken to their own homes, which by the looks of those lined up around her own, weren't going to be much better. Miss Hazel reached out to take her shoulders and turn her to face her.

"I know it's not as fancy as what you're used to, but a home is only what you make it. And now this is your home to make your own. When Elijah comes back from working this case, think about how wonderful it would it be for him to walk into a nice, clean house. He's been living here on his own, and considering he's a man, I have to say this place is much cleaner than most I've seen." Miss Hazel was looking around and nodding in agreement with herself.

Rose didn't want to even try speaking in case she started to cry. Every time she'd start thinking she'd done the right thing coming out here, something else would slam into her. And she would start questioning everything again. Miss Hazel had taught them all how to clean and do laundry, along with the other wifely tasks like cooking. But she was sure even the great Miss Hazel wouldn't be able to make this into a comfortable home.

Rose had never had to worry about the cleaning or decorating. Everything was always done for her. Now she realized just how much she'd taken for granted.

Well, if this was to be her home, then she was just going to have to do her best. Maybe if she got to work, she'd be able to get rid of the nagging worry that kept creeping in.

She took a deep breath, and smiled at Miss Hazel. "I can do this. At least it isn't a big house I have to clean." She had to find some kind of positive thoughts from this whole situation.

"That's the spirit, dear. Now, I'm off to take the others to their homes. We're all close together here, so you'll never really be alone. And we'll all meet for dinner this evening."

With that, Miss Hazel turned and walked out the door, closing it loudly behind her. The sound seemed deafening in the now empty room as Rose turned to look back at her new home.

The entire house was smaller than the parlor in her parent's home in Ottawa. There was a door off to the side, which she assumed led to a bedroom. She went over and opened the door slightly to peek inside. A large bed filled the center of the room, but there wasn't much else. A chair in one corner had some clothes slung over it, and a washstand sat on the other side.

Walking back into the main room, she looked for the door to the water closet. The only other door seemed to lead to the back of the home, into a central area between all the Mounties' houses. She walked over and opened it, smiling when she realized the other girls would be so close.

Outside, the lines stretched out for her to hang the laundry. But where was the water closet? She walked back toward the front of the house, and noticed a small building outside the window a ways from the house.

Surely she wasn't going to have to use an outhouse!

She opened the front door and looked at the rundown building. It looked like it was ready to blow over in the breeze. She quickly closed the door and fell back, leaning against it. She'd never had to use an outhouse before, but she'd heard of them. There was no way she could do this.

First, Theodore tells them to stay away from wild animals. Then these men expected them to use an outhouse, which required walking alone outside, where any of these wild animals could eat them alive.

"All right, Rose. You can do this. Miss Hazel wouldn't have brought you here if she didn't think you could do it. Remember what your other options are." Rose talked out loud to herself, hoping her voice could offer her some sort of reassurance.

No matter what, she wasn't ever going to go back and be stuck marrying Robert. He had tried to ruin her reputation and force her into the marriage he knew she didn't want. The marriage her parents wanted her to go through with.

Well, she'd shown them all. And now she had a

chance to find something more with a man who could possibly love her for who she was. Seeing how Theodore had looked at Jess today had given Rose hope for her own future.

Miss Hazel seemed to know what she was doing, so she had to trust her.

For better or worse, this small little shack was now her home. So it was time to start making it hers.

~

SHE WAS sure she had blisters on top of her blisters. Her hands had never known such work, but for some reason the pain didn't seem to take anything away from the pride she was feeling.

She'd started cleaning yesterday, then after having breakfast with the other girls this morning, she'd gotten right back to cleaning. She'd even taken all the sheets off the bed and washed them just like Miss Hazel had taught her. Last night, while trying to sleep in her new surroundings, she'd felt like an intruder sleeping in someone else's bed. The scent of the man who lived here had remained on the pillow, and she'd found herself smiling as she imagined what he looked like.

She'd taken all the clothes she'd seen lying around

and washed them, then hung them out to dry. While she'd been hanging them on the line out back, her heart felt full as she'd listened to JoAnn sing from her own back door. All of the girls had formed a special friendship, and Rose was grateful to have them with her.

Of them all, Tilly had become the closest to her. After that day at Miss Hazel's, Tilly had stepped up and helped Rose every chance she got. She knew how to cook anything, and she made sure to share any secrets she could with Rose.

Even though Tilly didn't seem as excited about the notion of coming out here to marry as some of the other girls, Rose was sure she had her own reasons for doing it.

Rose stood now and looked around the room. Everything was clean, and she'd even picked some flowers she found just outside the door and set them in a glass on the table. She hoped Elijah would appreciate the job she'd done. Especially since she knew once she had to cook for him, he was going to be wishing he'd had a more suitable woman chosen for him.

Yawning, she reached behind and pushed on her back. Scrubbing floors on her hands and knees was even harder than she'd imagined. But as she looked around at the work she'd done, she felt a sense of accomplishment she'd never experienced before.

Wiping her hands on her apron, she decided to go and rest for a few moments on the bed. Then she'd get herself cleaned up and ready in case Elijah came home soon.

She would just rest her eyes for a moment…

CHAPTER 5

*E*lijah stood in the doorway of his house, unable to move. He'd never really thought of himself as an untidy man, but seeing how clean everything was now, made him realize maybe his opinion of himself had been a bit off.

There were even flowers sitting on the table. He appreciated the effort, even if he could tell they were a bouquet of Common Tansey weeds that grew around this area. Someday, he might have to mention the fact they were a noxious weed if she continued to pick them for their table.

Guilt had eaten at him while he'd been out chasing the outlaw, knowing the poor woman had come all this way to marry him, and he hadn't even been here to greet her when she arrived. He wouldn't blame her if she was spitting mad and had decided not to go through with the wedding.

He still wasn't even sure what he was feeling about the marriage himself. He hoped when he saw the woman, he'd just know if it was right or not. But he figured that was just wishful thinking. He could easily end up married to an angry shrew who made his life miserable.

He wondered where his new bride was, then figured she must be with the others. That would give him some time to get himself cleaned up before meeting her.

Quickly, he opened the door to the bedroom as he pulled off his red jacket with the other hand. Stopping in his tracks, he had one arm out and one still in as he realized there was a body lying in the middle of the bed. And that body was snoring louder than a drunk sleeping off a night of carousing in the jail cell.

But what his eyes were seeing had pushed the noise to the back of his mind. The woman lying on the bed was beautiful, with dark hair poking out from beneath a small kerchief she'd tied over it. Her face was covered with smudges of dirt, which looked out of place on her white skin beneath. She wore an apron over a fancy dress, and he wondered why she'd worn something so pretty to clean the house.

As he stood staring with his arm still tangled in his jacket, she stirred. Feeling like a kid with his hand caught in the candy jar, he tried to back out of the room before she caught him staring. However, his booted foot caught on a dustpan she'd obviously forgotten to move during her cleaning. It clinked hard against the floor, causing the woman to bolt upright in the bed.

He'd never been so embarrassed in his life as he realized he was standing stock-still in horror, staring at the once sleeping woman with his coat half off.

"You must be Rose."

He squeezed his eyes shut briefly and groaned to himself. That wasn't the most romantic greeting he could have given her.

She struggled to get off the bed, obviously mortified at the situation. As she did, her feet got tangled in her skirt, and he watched in disbelief as she started to fall forward. He jumped into action and managed to reach her before she landed face down on the hard floor. Grabbing her arm, he took the brunt of it, falling backward with her on top of him.

If anyone had walked in, he was sure they'd have been horrified at what they were witnessing. A half-asleep woman lying on top of a man with his coat hanging off.

She lifted her head, and the breath flew from his lungs. Her eyes were as dark as her hair, and they seemed to be too large for her face as she looked at him. He could see the wetness of tears that were threatening to fall from embarrassment.

"I'm so sorry. I never...I mean, I was just going to lie down for a moment and rest my back a bit. I didn't think you'd be home yet, and I hoped to get myself cleaned up a bit before you had to meet me." He had to smile at the complete shock that was obvious in her voice.

"Well, this wasn't quite the greeting I was expecting, but I can't complain. I can think of worse things than having a beautiful woman landing on top of me."

As soon as he said the words, she pushed at his chest, trying to get herself upright. He wanted to hold on to her for a bit longer, but figured since they weren't technically married yet, he really couldn't do that.

She pushed away, promptly bringing her knee down hard on his groin. He groaned loudly, squeezing his eyes hard against the pain that erupted through his body. He vaguely heard her gasp, before she knelt back down beside him. "Oh my goodness, are you all right? Can I get you something?"

He swallowed hard, still not sure he could speak. He shook his head, and let his eyes open slowly. "No, I'm fine. I think it might be safer if you were to just stand over there for a bit until I can get myself up." His voice sounded croaky and uneven as he brought his lips together to take a few deep breaths.

When he was finally able to open his eyes fully, she was standing to the side of the room, wringing her hands together with worry. She looked like she was fighting hard to keep the tears from spilling over, and even from where he was still lying on the floor, he could see her lip trembling.

He felt like a heel. He didn't mean to upset her, and he knew how embarrassed she had to be feeling. She'd come all this way to meet a stranger and marry him, and he'd just told her to stand far away from him so it would be safer.

He needed to let her know there was nothing to feel embarrassed about. Struggling not to let the pain win, he carefully stood up and smiled at her. He reached his hand out to take hers and bring it up to his lips.

"Rose, it's wonderful to finally meet you."

Her eyebrows came together in confusion.

"My name is Elijah Thorpe, the man Miss Hazel has decided you should marry. I only hope I can be worthy of you coming all this way to meet me."

Her lips were parted slightly, and she tipped her head to the side as she watched him warily.

"I'd really hoped to be better dressed and fixed up before you met me." Her cheeks turned a bright shade of red as she looked up at him standing in front of her.

"Well, I have to say I think you're just about the prettiest girl I've seen this side of the Rockies, so I'm not sure there's much else you'd be able to do to look any nicer."

He realized the truth in the words as he spoke them. She was beautiful, even with the smudges and wrinkled clothes.

But the way she was now looking at him sideways, with one eyebrow slightly higher than the other, he was sure she didn't quite believe him.

"So, Rose, are you ready to get married?"

CHAPTER 6

"*Y*ou may kiss the bride."

The words echoed in her head as she looked up at the man in front of her. He was grinning at her, and she wasn't quite sure what she was supposed to do. Well, she knew what she was supposed to do—she just wasn't sure if she should.

Elijah brought his head closer and smiled as he gently brushed his lips over hers. As soon as they touched, a shock went through her body. When he pulled back, he looked into her eyes, bringing his eyebrows together as though he was confused about something.

But she couldn't worry about him. She had her own confusion to work out.

She had just married a complete stranger—a man

who she'd promptly fallen on top of and kneed in the groin upon meeting.

"Oh, congratulations, you two. I just *knew* it was a good match." Miss Hazel came from behind them where she'd witnessed their marriage and grabbed them both into a hug.

Rose pulled back from Elijah's arms and smiled at Miss Hazel. "Well, just because we're married, doesn't necessarily mean we're a good match. It will take a bit more time than a marriage ceremony to prove it one way or the other."

Elijah chuckled. "You're right about that. I still haven't even tasted her cooking." He winked at her, and Rose was sure he would be able to hear her heart beating above the noise of everything around them. Why did he have to mention the one thing she knew she couldn't do?

"That's true. And perhaps being married to a man who spends his days chasing outlaws instead of greeting a woman who's traveled hundreds of miles to meet him will turn out to be too much for me."

She smiled sweetly at him. She wasn't sure why she felt the need to make him feel bad about that, especially since it wasn't like he knew she couldn't cook. And, it wasn't like he had any control over the fact he was out working an assignment when she arrived.

But at the moment, her emotions were all over the place so she couldn't be responsible for anything she might say.

"Now you both can have the evening together getting to know each other. I'm sure Rose can put together a wonderful meal for you to share." Miss Hazel gave her a reassuring smile. "I have to go tend to other matters, and I'm sure you don't want me hanging around." Before Rose could beg Hazel to stay, the older woman was lifting her skirts and headed back up the street toward the Mounties' houses.

"I can honestly say I've never met a woman quite like Hazel Hughes. If I had half the authority in my voice she does, I'd have no trouble making outlaws and thieves cower before me."

Rose peered up at the man beside her. She smiled to herself at the look on his face as he watched Hazel walk away. It was a combination of awe and disbelief. That's how most people felt when they spoke with Hazel Hughes. It was almost as though she could convince someone to do anything she decided, whether they wanted to or not. Somehow, she always managed to get her way.

Rose let herself have a moment to take in the man she'd just married. He was tall, and she had to admit her stomach had butterflies when she looked at him. She'd never believed herself to be the type of girl swayed by a handsome man, but the way he looked in his red serge jacket did strange things to her insides.

One of the first things she'd noticed about him as she'd lain sprawled on top of him on the floor, was the blueness of his eyes as he'd looked at her. She could sense a kindness in their depths that seemed to reach in and tug at her heart somehow. She knew she was going to have to be careful around him until she was sure he was the kind of man she could trust.

And that he wouldn't be worse than the man she'd left behind in Ottawa.

They started heading up the street behind Hazel. The sun was starting to make its descent behind the mountains, leaving an orange glow around them. Her stomach grumbled as though to remind her it was past time for dinner.

After being completely mortified at how she'd met her future husband, Rose hadn't felt much like eating before they got cleaned up to get married. She would have loved a bath, but she didn't want to ask him to wait while she figured out how to get the tub inside and fill it with water. And she refused to ask him to do it after having just made a fool of herself in front of him.

So she'd quickly washed, changed, and brushed her hair while he put on a clean jacket. The next thing she knew, Miss Hazel was following them to see the preacher so they could be married.

Rose had no doubt the shock of their meeting had muddled her thinking. Until that disaster, she'd planned to have him wait at least a few days to get married so she could get to know him a bit better.

"Rose?"

She jumped as she realized Elijah had been talking to her.

"I'm sorry. My mind is just a bit of a mess right now." She may as well be honest with him. It wasn't like he hadn't already seen her at her worst.

He chuckled softly. "I can understand. I'll admit I'm a bit shaken up too. It's not every day I marry a woman I've only known a few hours." She looked over at him walking beside her and was relieved to see him smiling at her. She guessed getting married was just as scary for a man as it was for the woman sometimes.

His blue eyes found hers again. "I was just asking why a woman as pretty as you would need to come all the way out here to find a husband? I'm sure you must have had your choice of men back home."

She wasn't ready to tell him everything about herself. She still wanted him to see her for who she was, and not for the wealth her family had. All her life, she'd been the daughter of Andrew and Jane Lambert—one of the wealthiest families in Ottawa. Every man who'd ever paid her any attention wanted her for what she could give them.

This time, she hoped maybe the man beside her could see her for more than that. She pulled her lip in with her teeth and chewed on it as she worried that she might not have anything more to offer him. Maybe that's all she *did* have to give a man.

She shrugged. "There weren't a lot of good men to choose from where I grew up."

His eyebrow shot up. "Didn't you come from Ottawa too?"

"Well yes, but I was in an area without a lot of men." She knew it sounded ridiculous as soon as she said it. She needed to change the subject over to him.

"What about you? You're a strong, good-looking Mountie. Surely you could have your choice of women?"

His lips pulled up into a grin. "So you think I'm

good-looking? That's a relief. I was worried you'd go running for the woods when you met me."

She could already see she was going to have to be careful what she said around this man.

"Well, you're not the hideous, bald and short, bachelor Mountie I had pictured who'd need to send away for a bride. You could have been worse."

She realized she was actually joking around with a man without fearing she'd say the wrong thing. And she was surprised at how much she was enjoying it.

"*Could have been worse*…four words every man dreams of hearing from his new bride."

They continued walking, with Elijah pointing out different landmarks and buildings he thought she should know about, until they finally reached the door to their house. It felt so strange to be thinking of it as their house.

Suddenly, her stomach started to churn as she realized she was going to be alone in this house with her new husband. How was she supposed to act? She stopped breathing as the next question pushed its way into her worried mind.

Where would they sleep?

CHAPTER 7

*E*lijah watched as Rose worked at the stove. She'd seemed to be relaxing around him a bit as they'd walked home earlier, but since they'd gotten here, she'd been a bundle of nerves. He knew this was an unusual situation for them both, so he could understand her apprehension.

When they came inside, he'd gotten the fire going so she could start cooking. She worked at putting together something in a pan while he went in to change into his everyday clothes.

They talked a bit while she finished preparing the meal to go in the oven. He told her he needed to chop some wood, hoping it would give him a chance to get his wits about himself. Having a woman standing in his kitchen was hard to get used to.

After a while, he went back inside and couldn't see her anywhere. He stood there, unsure what to do, until his bedroom door opened. Rose came out wearing a ruffled blouse and skirt that was more elegant than anything he'd seen most women wear around here, even on Sundays.

"I forgot to change my clothes when I got home." She smiled shyly at him as she went over and took the apron down to put over her clothes.

"Do you not have anything more suitable to wear out here?" He cringed as soon as the words left his lips because he realized it sounded like he didn't like how she was dressed. She swung her gaze over to him and creased her forehead.

"Is there something wrong with that I'm wearing?" She sounded annoyed as she looked down at her attire.

"Well, I can't imagine the fabric would hold up well against the elements out here. Most women wear more sensible clothes that will withstand the day to day cooking, cleaning, and chores women are supposed to do."

He clenched his jaw tight to stop himself from talking any more. It seemed like every time he tried to say something, it came out completely wrong. He could tell by the way her eyes were squinted and the redness of her cheeks as she glared at him that she was angry with his choice of words.

"Sensible? I'll have you know, nothing I've done in the past few weeks has been *sensible*. And now you have the nerve to tell me my clothing is lacking as well? These garments are the top fashions of today, and most women would kill to have them in their closets. I chose only the best ones to bring, hoping it would help to make a good impression on you. But apparently, you would prefer if I wore something a bit more *sensible*."

She had stopped back over by the stove and was now holding a pan in her hands as she walked toward him. He honestly started to worry that she was going to hit him with it, and he'd have to arrest his own wife for battery on an officer of the law.

He swallowed hard, determined not to say another word. She stood in front of him, chest heaving as she struggled to get her anger under control. This was exactly why he'd sworn to never get married. Most married men he knew had to deal with irrational wives who got upset at the simplest of things.

How could he have forgotten all of that? Between

Miss Hazel's persuasiveness in telling him he needed a wife, and Rose's beauty when he met her, he'd been blinded.

Suddenly, a large poof of smoke started to swirl out of the oven behind her. She hadn't noticed yet as she continued to glare in his direction, waiting for him to reply.

"Um...Rose? I think something's burning." He pushed past her to get to the stove before his entire house went up in flames.

She came rushing behind him, crashing into him when he stopped at the oven. "Oh no, my shepherd's pie!" She grabbed the pot holders from the cupboard beside the stove and flung the door open. Smoke quickly filled the room making them both cough and choke.

As she pulled the charred pan from the oven, she tried to set it on top. But with a scream, she ended up dropping the entire mess onto the floor. They both stood looking at the black mound that sat smoking between them.

Finally, she lifted her eyes to his and he noticed her blinking quickly. Her mouth opened to speak, but no words came out. Turning, she ran to the bedroom and slammed the door. The sound hit him like a train as he realized how hard these past few days had been on her. And today had been a complete mess right from the moment they met.

He'd be surprised if she didn't pack her bags and catch the first train out of Squirrel Ridge Junction. Maybe it would be best for them both if she did.

But as he kept his gaze on the now closed door to the bedroom he'd been sleeping in since he was posted here, he realized a part of him was really hoping she'd still want to stay.

∼

"I'm sure you're making everything sound much worse than it really was Rose. Elijah seems like a nice man, I'm sure he will understand."

Tilly patted her hand as the women sat around the table listening to her. Tilly, Evelyn, and Rose had met at Jess and Theodore's for a visit while the men went in to write out the report about the outlaw who was still on the loose.

"No, it wouldn't surprise me if he isn't over talking to the preacher before he leaves to see if there's a way he could get out of this marriage. I've always been a bit unsteady and perhaps a touch clumsy in my life, but never have I carried on like I did yesterday when I met him." She ignored the looks the ladies gave each other as she mentioned that she was a touch clumsy. She knew they'd witnessed her unusual knack for making a complete mess out of the simplest of things on more than one occasion.

"Then, as if that wasn't enough, he told me my clothes aren't sensible for living out here. While I was losing my temper with him, I almost proceeded to burn his house down." She buried her head in her hands while the others offered their sympathies.

"I tried to cook it the way you showed me, Tilly. But it seems that no matter how hard I try, making anything that is even close to edible is going to be an impossible task for me. The poor man is stuck with a woman who can dress fancy, but can't even cook him a simple meal."

She'd lain in bed last night, listening to the new sounds outside her window, while she tried to talk herself out of running back home to Ottawa. Every time she went over in her mind what had happened within the short time since she'd met her new husband, she'd cringed with embarrassment and shame.

And after running into the bedroom after the disaster with the food, she'd heard him quietly cleaning everything up. Then he hadn't even bothered trying to come in to sleep in his own bed, giving her the time she needed to sort her feelings out. She had no doubt many men would have insisted sleeping there as was their right as a husband.

She assumed he'd slept on the floor somewhere, and that was something else that made her feel guilty. Shame over how she'd acted had caused her to hide in the bedroom this morning until she heard him leave, so he'd had to make his own breakfast. When she'd come out, a plate of food for her was left on the table covered with another plate to keep it warm.

She needed to pick herself up and do what needed to be done—and that was being a good wife to the man she'd married. It wasn't fair to him that he was being made to suffer because she'd decided she didn't want to stay in Ottawa anymore.

Just as she'd wiped her eyes and smiled at the women around her, ready to announce her intentions to give it another try to make things work, the door to Jess's house opened. And the men all walked through the door behind Theodore.

They were all handsome enough men, but Rose's eyes found Elijah immediately and her heart soared when he offered her a kind smile. He didn't seem angry with her, when she knew he had every right.

She wasn't even paying attention now to what the others were doing as she watched Elijah walk straight over to her at the table.

"How are you this morning, Rose? Did you sleep all right?"

She nodded, offering him a shy smile. "I did. I didn't hear you get up this morning, but thank you for the breakfast. I was hungry." She couldn't admit to him she'd been awake and hiding from him.

"Would you like to go for a ride today so I can show you around your new home? There's a lot to see around Squirrel Ridge Junction, and since Theodore is letting me have the day off, I thought we could see some of the area together."

As she looked up at him smiling down at her, with his curl hanging in his eyes, she realized in all her life she'd never known a man to be this kind to her, and not expect anything from her in return.

He didn't know how wealthy she was, and he didn't seem to care she wasn't quite the ideal wife material either. He still wanted to give her a chance and get to know her.

She stood up from the table, reaching out to take his hand he was holding out for her.

"There's nothing I would like more."

CHAPTER 8

"*E*verything is so different here. Even the air just seems fresher." She looked around and took a deep breath in. "In Ottawa, there always seems to be a lot of dust and dirt, and people everywhere you look. It's kind of nice to be able to get away and see how beautiful the world can be."

She'd never seen trees so green and grass so lush. And every time her eyes made their way to the mountains in the distance, it took her breath away.

"Yes, it took me a while to get used to the mountains. They made me feel closed in when I first arrived in British Columbia."

She looked over at the man riding on the large black horse beside her. His horse stood a great deal taller than hers, so she found herself having to tilt her head up to see him.

"Where did you come from?"

"Manitoba. The ground is as flat as a board and you can see for miles in every direction. It was hard to get used to not being able to see the horizon on all sides."

"Is your family still there?" She was enjoying the chance to get to know him without having to worry about cooking or anything that might ruin the moment.

"My grandma is still there. She's getting older, and I worry about her being back there all alone, but she insisted I follow my calling and not to worry about her."

"Where are your parents?" As soon as she asked, she wished she could take the words back. Obviously if he wanted to talk about his parents, he would have mentioned them.

He kept his eyes on the green hills ahead of them and shrugged. "My father was gunned down after a stagecoach robbery when I was a boy. My mom died shortly after. My grandma always said she died from a broken heart."

"Oh my goodness. That's awful!"

"She always knew what could happen. You see, my dad was one of the first Mounties in the area and he lived and breathed the law. That's why I knew I had to do what my father had believed in, and died for."

Her heart was pounding as she imagined Elijah's poor mother, losing the man she loved.

Seeing the way he was clenching his jaw and how he was sitting so stiff in his saddle, she realized he was going back to the sadness of his past. She wanted to do something to bring him back to here and take his mind off it.

"Race you to that tree." As she said the words, she grinned in his direction.

His head whipped to look at her, and his eyebrows were pulled sharply together in shock. When his mouth opened to speak, she laughed and kicked her heels in, leaving him coughing in a cloud of dust.

She raced toward the tree, letting herself revel in the feeling of the wind blowing her hair out behind her. This was something that would never have been allowed in Ottawa. She wasn't even sure if it was allowed here, but at the moment, she didn't care.

When she got to the tree she'd spotted, she pulled on the reins and turned to see how far behind her he was. She was stunned to see him reining in right behind her. His face was red with exertion; and she braced herself for him to yell at her.

"Do you realize how dangerous it is to be riding like a madwoman across open ground that you're not familiar with? What if something had spooked your horse, or it had stepped in a hole?"

He didn't really sound as angry as she was expecting, but he wasn't happy with her either.

"Well, I'm fine. Nothing happened, so you don't need to be mad. I just thought it might be fun to have a little race but I guess I was wrong." She was getting really annoyed at his attitude all of a sudden. Here she was trying to have some fun, and lighten the mood a bit, and he decided to yell at her like a child.

"Where did you learn to ride like that? It's not every day you see a woman who can hop on a horse and ride like you can. I'd assumed from your clothes and lack of skills in the kitchen, you'd most likely had a fairly pampered life."

She remembered hearing the expression about seeing red one time, but hadn't really understood what it meant.

Until now.

Clenching her jaw tightly so she could keep her words calm, she pinned her glare on him. She vaguely noticed he was cringing, obviously aware that he may have worded his sentence wrong. But she didn't care if he was feeling remorseful.

"I may have led a somewhat pampered life as you so kindly put it, however I did manage to get away sometimes and do things I enjoyed. My father paid for riding lessons, but he didn't realize just how much I would sneak away for a ride with my friend. I'm quite skilled on a horse, as opposed to my lack in the kitchen."

Her breathing was coming in short, hard gasps as she fought to control her anger. He pushed his hand hard through his hair and looked down sheepishly.

"I'm sorry, that's not what I meant. It didn't come out right."

"No, it didn't. I am sorry you ended up with a wife who is a bit less able in the kitchen than Jess and Tilly are, but I'm trying to learn. I came all the way here hoping for a chance to make a life for myself somewhere far away from what I'd grown up with, and nothing seems to be working out the way I'd hoped. I admit rushing into marriage with a stranger might not have been my smartest choice, but at the time I really didn't have many other options."

He was staring at her now with his mouth half-open as though he wanted to speak but was afraid to say anything else that might set her off more.

"Do you know what it's like to spend your whole life being told how to act, what to wear, who to talk to, and who to marry? Can you imagine no one listening to you when you say you want something different? I'm tired of being treated like I can't think for myself." She spun her horse around, but before kicking in her heels, she looked him in the eye.

"If I want to ride my horse like a madwoman, I will go ahead and do it. I dare you to try and stop me."

She raced back toward town, and didn't care if Elijah was following her or not. She'd never spoken like that to anyone before in her life, and she felt a twinge of guilt to have taken it out on her new husband.

But maybe now he'd learn to think before he spoke.

CHAPTER 9

"So, what did you do to Rose to get her so fired up?" Miss Hazel stood directly in front of him with her hand on her hip and her eyes wrinkled together. "That girl has always been so sweet and kindhearted, I've never seen her so spitting mad."

"What makes you think I did anything? She just took something I said the wrong way and got all riled up." He was scared to admit the truth to Hazel. He was sure she'd grab him by the ear and drag him behind a tree to put him across her knee.

He was supposed to be the big, strong Mountie, yet here he was afraid to be scolded by a feisty, older woman.

He felt bad enough for what he'd said to his new wife. It seemed when he was around Rose, he always ended up saying things wrong. But he'd been worried when he saw her go tearing across the field like she had, without giving him any warning. For all he knew, her horse had gone crazy and she couldn't get it under control.

She really shouldn't blame him, considering how she'd managed to fall on him, knee him somewhere that was still tender, and almost burn his house down within a few short hours. So of course he'd be nervous with her on top of a horse.

"Well, what are you going to do to fix it?" Miss Hazel wasn't happy with him, and she wasn't going to let him go until he gave in.

They had just come out of church, and the others were all standing around talking. Rose had barely spoken two words to him since he'd gotten back yesterday. They'd all gone and had dinner together, listening to Kendall and JoAnn singing last night, so Rose had managed to avoid being alone with him.

She'd gone straight to bed when they got home, while he curled up on the floor once again.

This morning, she'd gotten up and made them pancakes and bacon for breakfast. The pancakes had been sticky and as thick as mud, with about as much flavor. And the bacon had been burned to a black charcoal color.

But he'd eaten it with a smile and told her it was delicious.

He looked over at her, and she was looking at him while she talked to Nolan's new wife, Tilly. As soon as their eyes met, she quickly turned her head away.

What was it about this woman that had already gotten under his skin? Why should he even care if she was angry with him? Truthfully, he could send her back home any time if he really wanted to.

But for some reason he couldn't quite figure out, he knew he didn't want to send her away. Even if the sane part of him said it would likely be for his own safety.

And he didn't want her to be mad at him.

Coming back to the conversation with Miss Hazel, he said, "I don't know yet, Miss Hazel. I will admit to being a bit confused about it all. Sometimes you women can be hard to figure out."

Her eyebrow went up and her head tilted to one side. "Is that so?"

In that moment, he realized, he was about to find out just how much he really did need to be more careful what he said around a woman.

"You know, I think your new husband is actually quite smitten with you. I hope you'll be patient with him. He's a quiet man, and sometimes he says things without thinking."

Rose shook the wrinkles out of the shirt, then hung it on the line. Miss Hazel was standing beside her, helping her hang the rest of the washing out. She'd stopped in for a visit this morning as soon as Elijah had left to go on his rounds. He'd be gone overnight again, so Rose had some time to try and figure out what she planned to do from here.

They'd spoken a bit over the rest of yesterday, but things were still strained. To be fair, Elijah had tried his best to make things right with her. Well, he'd done everything except actually apologize.

"Miss Hazel, do you truly believe I can make it out here? Especially since I grew up having everything done for me. And then, the fact that I'm a bit, well...you know."

Hazel squinted her eyes together and turned to face her, putting her hands on her hips. "Rose Thorpe, I don't think you've ever given yourself enough credit. You're a strong woman, but you've never had the chance to show anyone. So what if you're sometimes a bit like that silly moose I can see over there all tangled up in the clothesline behind Evelyn's house."

Rose peeked around the shirt she'd just hung, and let out a laugh at the sight she could see.

The moose that was always hanging around had his antlers caught in the clothesline, but he didn't seem in the least bothered by it. It would seem it was actually something he was quite used to doing. He happily continued eating the long grass around him, pulling the line farther down each time.

"Should someone go help him?" She was giggling now as she watched him. He lifted his head and looked at her while he chewed.

Hazel was shaking her head as she looked at him. "I don't know what it is about that moose, but he reminds me of a man I knew many years ago. My uncle, Monty Hughes. He was the kindest, most gentle soul I've ever known, and that man never cared a whit what anyone else thought about him. He was a bit of a blundering man, who could manage to trip over his own feet at least once a day."

The woman was smiling as she remembered the man she'd obviously loved a great deal. "But he'd also give you the shirt off his back if you needed it." She turned to look at Rose with a glint in her eye. "Even if he might accidentally knock you down while giving it to you."

Monty Hughes sounded a lot like herself.

Hazel looked back at the moose as he started to walk over to another patch of grass, managing somehow to get himself untangled from the line. As he did, the line sprung back, flinging most of the clothes that poor Evelyn had already washed that morning halfway across the yard.

"I think we should call him Monty."

Hazel nodded, as though that had settled it.

Rose laughed as she continued watching the massive animal lumber across the grass to the next patch, as though he didn't have a care in the world and hadn't just destroyed a clothesline and a day's worth of washing.

"I think that's the perfect name for him. Monty the Moose. He may be a bit awkward and clumsy, but he quite obviously knows he belongs here."

Hazel reached out and patted her arm before reaching into the basket to grab some socks to hang on the line. "And hopefully soon, you'll realize that Monty isn't the only one who belongs here."

CHAPTER 10

"I'm sure going to miss that woman, even if she does manage to make me feel like an awkward child who needs to learn to mind his manners every time she's around me."

Elijah waved at the train that was pulling from the station carrying Miss Hazel back home. She'd arrived in town like a whirlwind once again, and left just as quickly. But this time, she'd left him with a wife he still wasn't sure how to manage. Over the past few days, they'd seemed to reach a quiet under-standing and had been slowly getting to know each other.

He still slept on his bedroll on the floor, which was beginning to take its toll on his back. He didn't mind sleeping on the hard ground when he was on overnight patrol, but what he wouldn't give for his own soft bed when he was home.

And he had to admit he'd been thinking about the woman he'd be sharing that bed with an awful lot too.

"Well, if I know Miss Hazel as well as I think I do, she will head back to Ottawa and start looking for the next group of women she can marry off to more poor Mounties who keep our great nation safe. Or, something along those lines, as she said when she cornered me in church not so long ago."

Rose smiled over at him as she turned from waving her goodbyes to the older woman.

They started walking back from the station, while the others all went their separate ways. Now that Miss Hazel was gone, it was up to all of them to make things work with their new wives. Rose's cooking hadn't gotten much better since she'd arrived, even though he knew Hazel and Tilly both had been offering their help. But he couldn't complain because he could see how hard she really was trying.

"I've been wondering how that conversation must have gone. What made you decide to travel all this way to marry a stranger anyway?"

She still wasn't giving him much information

about her past, other than the fact she'd grown up in Ottawa. Any time he tried to ask her about it, she would just brush it off.

Elijah's job as a Mountie was to always work to uncover the truth, but he was finding her to be a tough case to figure out.

He turned his head slightly to watch her as she kept her own gaze straight ahead. Finally, she gave a slight shrug and small laugh. "I didn't really have many options. When Miss Hazel came to me, I realized it was my chance to get away and try for a life of my own."

He sensed there was more to it, but he didn't want to push her too much. This was the most she'd ever opened up to him and as he kept his eyes on her, he could see by the redness of her cheeks, she was embarrassed at having shared as much as she had.

"Well, I'm glad Miss Hazel found you for me. I'm sure I got the prettiest bride by far."

Her head whipped around and her big eyes stared at him in shock. He wouldn't have believed her cheeks could get any redder, but as he watched, they changed to an almost purple color.

He had to admit, he was just as shocked at himself. He'd never been much for paying compliments to women, and hadn't really had the time to learn how to properly court a lady. Yet, with Rose, he found himself feeling like she would never reject him or do anything to hurt him. Maybe it was just because they were already married, so he knew he really had nothing to lose by trying.

Suddenly, she stopped and tilted her head to the side while watching him warily. Her eyebrows pulled together and she crossed her arms in front of her stomach. "Are you sure you wouldn't rather have a bride like Tilly who could cook for you without burning your house down?"

He laughed and waved his hand to the side. "You haven't actually burned it down yet."

She continued to look at him. "What about being as feisty and tough as Evelyn? She'd likely make life interesting for you."

He made his face into a cringe. "No, I'm not sure I'd be able to put up with what poor Joel has been dealing with. Besides, at least you've agreed to already marry me. He still doesn't know if he'll end up with a wife or not."

"Well, JoAnn is a lot of fun and can sing like an angel. If I were to try singing to you, you'd likely have to stuff cotton in your ears to keep from crying."

He chuckled. "I agree that JoAnn does have a beautiful voice."

When her face fell slightly, he had to smile to himself. For a woman as beautiful as Rose, she sure didn't see what she could have to offer a husband.

Reaching out, he took both of her hands in his. "But I'm enjoying getting to know the woman I married. The woman who keeps me on my toes and who I can sense has a goodness inside her that's never been able to shine through. A person who's brave and strong and willing to marry a man thousands of miles away from her home, just so she could have the chance to make a life of her own."

He smiled down at her as he watched her chest rise and fall with each breath.

"I know sometimes I might not say the right words, but I'm glad you came to Squirrel Ridge Junction, and I'm glad you agreed to be my wife. Even if we have done things a bit backward."

"What do you mean?"

His fingers reached up and pushed back a strand of hair that had fallen forward onto her cheek. The smoothness of her skin beneath his rough fingers set his whole body on fire. He watched as she swallowed slowly, never taking her eyes from his face.

"I mean, every woman deserves to be courted

properly. Especially you, Rose. So, I'd like you to accept my intention to court you the way you should be."

Somehow, Elijah knew the woman he'd married deserved a proper courtship. He hadn't planned it until this moment, seeing her so unsure of her place and what he wanted from a wife.

He wanted to make this work. And he hoped theirs could be a true marriage.

But even as he said the words, he had to push the niggling worry that always reared its ugly head. Being a Mountie was dangerous. He'd found that out at a young age.

What happened if Rose fell in love with him, only to end up widowed like his ma had been? What if they had children, and he left them without a father?

He'd always swore he'd never let it happen. Yet here he was, married to a beautiful woman and finding himself drawn into the depths of those dark eyes staring into his own.

Somehow though, as they stood on the street lost in each other's eyes, he sensed they both needed each other more than they knew.

And for reasons he couldn't understand, he already knew he could never let her go.

CHAPTER 11

"Thank you so much, Tilly. I can't believe I've managed to make all of this food without anything coming out the color of coal. Not to mention tasting like it too." Rose shook her head in disbelief as she stared at the roast chicken, boiled potatoes, carrots, and apple pie. "Although I guess I can believe it since you really told me what to do every step of the way."

Tilly laughed and shook her head. "Rose, you're getting better. It's not something a person can learn overnight. You've never had to do it for yourself, so you need to just be patient. It will come."

Rose lifted her head and smiled at her friend. Tilly had become someone she knew she could trust and confide in, and spending the day cooking with her had been a wonderful distraction. Rose had no expectations of ever becoming a world class chef, but she did hope she could at least learn to cook for her husband without serious incident.

"Elijah will be so surprised when he gets home from his overnight patrol."

"I still think it is so romantic that he has declared his intentions to court you. He didn't have to do that, since technically you both are already married. I have to say, these Mounties we've married are true gentlemen, even if things have been a serious adjustment to what we were used to."

Rose laughed quietly. "I'd say serious adjustment was a bit of an understatement."

Tilly came over and patted her on the shoulder. "You're adjusting remarkably well. I'd say in no time you'll be madly in love with Elijah and your old life back in Ottawa will be nothing but a distant memory."

Rose smiled at her friend. "I wish the same for you too, Tilly. You and Nolan seem perfect together, so I'm sure you're soon going to be able to put your own past behind you." Even though, she didn't know all of the details, Rose knew enough to know Tilly was running from something painful.

The door opened and Elijah stood silhouetted with the light of the setting sun behind him. Tilly started to grab her things she'd brought to help Rose, while quickly shooting a subtle wink in her direction.

Rose's heart was pounding wildly as she looked at her husband. His hair was tousled even more than normal from the days he'd been on patrol. He looked tired, but his eyes instantly searched for her. Her pulse quickened as his eyes met hers and he smiled.

Robert, the man everyone had always assumed she would marry, had never been able to make her feel like this. Even though every woman in Ottawa was throwing themselves at his feet, Rose had never seen what the attraction was.

He'd been confident, arrogant, and smug while Elijah was quietly sure of himself, without feeling the need to make anyone feel he was better than them. And as far as Rose was concerned, Elijah was much better looking. Seeing him in his red jacket as he pulled his arms from the sleeves, her knees suddenly felt weak. She was sure if she tried to speak her voice would crack.

Thankfully, Tilly was on her way to the door, smiling at Elijah. "I hope you don't mind that I spent the day here with Rose. It's nice to have a friend to be able to spend time with."

"Not at all. You're welcome here any time, Tilly. I

have to say I feel a bit sorry for you knowing how hungry Nolan will likely be since we've been on our patrol. Even though he still eats more than a horse of the food we've made over the fire, it's obvious he's become used to a more satisfying fare."

Tilly laughed softly. "Well, I better get myself home then so I can make sure he's fed." She turned to wave to Rose, who was still standing there nervously waiting for Elijah to come inside and see everything she'd cooked. "I will see you tomorrow."

Elijah came inside and pulled his jacket the rest of the way off, throwing it over the back of the chair at the table. "It smells wonderful in here, Rose. Did you make all this?" His voice sounded surprised as he walked over and peeked over her shoulder, looking at the food sitting on the counter.

She bit her tongue from scolding him for not believing she was capable of making a meal. It wouldn't really be fair to be mad at him considering it was mostly true.

"Tilly helped me, but I tried to do most of it." She was feeling a strange sense of pride at having accomplished such an everyday task, even if she was doubtful she could have done it on her own. But seeing the smile on Elijah's face warmed her heart.

Since the day he'd announced he was going to

officially court her, he'd gone out of his way to follow through on his promise. They'd gone for walks, ridden around Squirrel Ridge Junction while he showed her the beauty of British Columbia, and spent a few evenings at the homes of the other Mounties. She hoped that tonight she'd have the courage to tell him everything about why she came west.

She was starting to believe he could perhaps be someone who could possibly care for her and not just her family's wealth.

But she also knew she had to tell him about the scandal that had set everything in motion in the first place. She hoped he'd believe her and understand why she had to leave Ottawa.

He leaned over to sniff at the still warm pie, closing his eyes as he let the scent fill his nose. "Oh, this smells heavenly. I've heard rumors that Tilly knows how to make the best pies."

Rose swallowed hard. "Actually, I made this one. Tilly just told me what to do." The words came out angrier than she'd planned, but for some reason, hearing him talk about how good Tilly's pies were had stung.

His head whipped up, and he nodded quickly. "No, I know you made it. I'm sure it will be perfect."

She had to take pity on him. The look on his face as he tried to figure out what he'd said wrong was endearing, so she couldn't be mad. She'd started to learn over the past week that sometimes he had a hard time finding the right words to express what he wanted to say.

She wanted tonight to be perfect. He had somehow managed find his way into her heart, and she was determined to make things work with this awkward Mountie who didn't seem to mind that he didn't get a bride who could cook.

She decided it didn't just have to be the man who did the courting.

CHAPTER 12

"*R*ose, this is delicious. Honestly, I don't think even my grandmother makes apple pie this good." He lifted his eyes quickly and opened them wide in mock horror. "But don't you dare tell her I said that!"

"I will keep your secret. Especially since I can't promise you will ever get another one that tastes this good unless Tilly comes over and helps me cook every day." Rose laughed as she took another bite of her own pie. It really was heavenly.

Elijah just shrugged as he smiled across the table at her. "I think you might surprise yourself. And even if you never made another dish that tasted like this, I can't complain. I have the most beautiful woman sitting across the table to share my meals with, so I'm a happy man."

She could feel her cheeks start to burn as he nonchalantly looked back at his pie to take another bite. She had to give him credit—he seemed to know what to say to make a woman happy. He'd obviously been raised right.

"So, do you get to visit your grandmother often?" She remembered him mentioning his grandma living in Manitoba when they'd been on their ride that day, before they'd ended up arguing.

He shook his head and gave a sad smile. "Not as often as I'd like. She writes me letters every week, though, to let me know what she's up to, and I write back to tell her what I'm doing." He leaned back in his chair, having finished his pie. "I imagine I'm going to be getting a fairly long one scolding me for not letting her be here for my wedding."

"I hope she isn't too angry with you. And that she approves when I finally get to meet her." For some reason, getting the approval from this woman she'd never met had suddenly become very important to Rose.

He absently pushed at the curl that hung down while he studied her. Finally, he nodded. "Oh, I'm sure she'll approve. She'd given up on me marrying."

"Why did she think you wouldn't marry?"

He looked past her and shrugged. "After my ma

died from missing my father so deeply, I'd always told my grandma I would never do that to a woman. It wasn't fair to be married to a Mountie, who could be taken from them so easily."

Rose held her breath as she realized the truth in his words. She'd known marrying a Mountie had risks, but she hadn't really let herself think about it much. What if she did let herself fall in love with this man, only to have him ripped from her arms and left alone to grieve?

"So, what changed your mind?" Her voice shook as she spoke quietly into the room.

His eyes came back to hers and he smiled. "Well, you've met Miss Hazel…"

She laughed, letting out the breath she'd been holding. "Of course. Miss Hazel doesn't exactly take no for an answer."

"What about you, Rose? You haven't told me anything about your reasons for coming all the way here to marry a stranger. A woman as beautiful as you must have had suitors lined up outside your door. So why come all the way here?"

She stood up to clear the dishes from the table, feeling uncomfortable as he watched her intently. "I didn't have a lot of suitors. I kept to myself a lot and just didn't want to be stuck living in Ottawa for the rest of my life. I'd always hoped to have more, so when Miss Hazel approached me, I knew it was my chance."

Why couldn't she just tell him the truth?

That she came from one of the wealthiest families in Ottawa, and had never had any say in anything she did in her life. That she'd been engaged to a man she never wanted to marry, and he'd promptly ruined her reputation when he realized she was planning to call off their engagement.

Elijah didn't seem the kind of man to judge her harshly for her past, so she couldn't understand what was stopping her from telling him everything.

He was following her with his eyes as she moved to set the dishes into the wash basin on the counter. "I find it had to believe you didn't have any suitors at all. There must have been someone. And what about your parents? Were they angry about you coming out here to marry a strange man? I'd think they'd have wanted to be here for your marriage."

When he asked the question, she promptly dropped a dish on the floor as she turned sharply back to the counter. It shattered with a loud crash, sending shards of porcelain all over the wooden floor.

She hurriedly crouched down to start picking up

the pieces, hearing his chair push back against the floorboards as he came over to help. He bent down and she caught a glimpse of his blue eyes as he looked over at her.

"I'm so sorry, Elijah. Honestly, I don't know why I'm so fumble-fingered all the time. You'll have nothing left to your house with me around."

He smiled. "It's our house now, Rose. And I'd be happy enough if there was nothing left but you."

The few pieces she'd already picked up fell to the floor once again as she heard him speak. When he reached out and lightly brushed his fingers along her cheek, she finally understood what it could feel like to have someone care for her. She'd never known anyone to look at her the way Elijah was at this moment.

Swallowing hard, she quickly stood up. She wasn't used to having anyone pay her compliments without it seeming empty and only offered to her because they knew who her family was.

Elijah rose too, reaching out and taking her hands in his. "Rose, I know we both ended up in a marriage we maybe weren't sure of, or how it even happened. But maybe Miss Hazel knows more than we know. I do know that since you've arrived, I've found myself being much more excited to come home, knowing you'll be here. And even though my back is aching from sleeping on a hard floor, I look forward to having you here in the morning to share my table with." He grinned at her as he gently rubbed his thumbs over her hands. "I will even admit to almost looking forward to seeing how my food will taste each day."

She laughed nervously, having a hard time concentrating while his thumbs left a burning trail over her skin.

Her pulse raced as his eyes bore into hers, sending her heart into a tailspin. Robert had never made her feel like this. When he'd touched her, she'd felt her skin crawl. The way Elijah's skin felt on hers made her whole body heat up.

Just as she was sure her knees would give out under her, Elijah brought his head down and his lips softly touched hers. He held her hands firmly between them, and pulled them up to press against his chest. She could feel his heart pounding against his chest as one hand came free to reach around her back, pulling her in closer.

As his lips moved over hers, she was grateful for the support his arm was giving her. His other hand was still holding hers, tucked between them as though he was afraid she'd try to get away if he didn't hold her tight.

She knew at this moment she'd never try to get away.

When he pulled back, she had to force her eyes back open. Her lips were still parted slightly and she was sure the room around her was spinning slowly.

He smiled down at her as he reached up and caressed her bottom lip. "Yes, I'd say Miss Hazel might have known exactly what she was doing."

CHAPTER 13

*E*lijah rode back into town, saying hello to people who were stopping to tell them how much fun they'd had at the reception the night before. The community didn't get to celebrate often, so when they'd had the opportunity to come out for the marriage reception of the town Mounties, it had been a night of revelry and excitement.

Of course, it had been planned for a while, but the reception hadn't been able to happen until all of the couples were married, and since Joel had dragged his feet until yesterday, the reception had been on hold until then.

He smiled as he remembered the smile Rose had wore all evening, even after her incident with the cake she'd offered to make. After having it end up on the floor, she'd been devastated at not being able to take it to the reception.

But, he'd spun her around on the dance floor and enjoyed the feeling of having her in his arms all night.

He hadn't been happy about having to go out and deal with a squabble among some neighbors this morning who seemed unable to settle things themselves. He'd have far rather spent the morning sitting with his wife.

Elijah couldn't wait to get back home and see Rose. After the past couple of nights, getting to know his wife and spending more time with her, he was starting to let go of his doubts and worries, and was determined to follow his grandmother's advice. Whenever he'd say he didn't want to marry and leave his wife a widow, his grandma had clucked her tongue and shook her head, telling him he was being a fool.

He could hear her voice in his head. *"You can't spend your life without falling in love. Having someone love you, and who can share your life with you, is worth every moment of sadness you would feel if they left you. The same goes for any woman who loves you. There are always risks in life, and just because you're a Mountie, doesn't mean you should never allow a woman to love you. You never know what you would be missing if you don't give yourself the chance to feel love."*

Elijah wasn't sure what he was feeling for Rose at the moment, but he was starting to understand what his grandmother was always telling him.

As he rode into town, a cloud of dust following behind him, Elijah's heart jumped when he noticed a familiar black head of hair standing and talking with Joel and Evelyn outside the mercantile. She carried her basket with food she'd just picked up. Rose's eyes found his, a smile reaching across her face. Knowing she was just as happy to see him made his stomach pull into a knot.

Riding up beside her, he quickly dismounted and reached out for her hand. He didn't want to embarrass her by kissing her in front of everyone, so he simply lifted her fingers to his lips and grinned at her. "Hello, Rose."

He could almost feel Joel rolling his eyes behind him, but he didn't care. In that moment, his eyes only saw one person. And she was standing in front of him with her cheeks the color of fire.

Suddenly, the train could be heard pulling into the station up the street, breaking the moment between them. Since the train only came through once a week, when it arrived, it caused a lot of commotion. People raced to see what mail had come through, and to see if any new people would be arriving to stay in Squirrel Ridge Junction.

When they were around, the Mounties always made a point of being close by at the station in case things ever got out of hand.

"Guess we better head over to the station, Elijah." Joel was already moving in that direction, holding his wife's hand as they turned to go.

Rose fell into step beside Elijah with Evelyn on the other side of her,. As they neared the station where the train was still hissing like a great beast, he noticed the fancy Pullman car attached to the usual rail cars that made the run.

Whoever was in that car was definitely someone important. Elijah wondered why they hadn't been notified of anyone special arriving in town.

Suddenly, Rose stumbled beside him and gasped. "No."

One word, but it sent a chill down his spine. His head turned to her, and he noticed her skin had gone a deathly white. She'd gone stock-still and her eyes were large as she looked at the people stepping onto the platform from the car.

"Rose, are you all right?" He was more concerned

about his wife at the moment than who the important people were stepping off the train.

Before she could answer, a woman's voice called from the platform. "Rose! Oh, Rose, how good it is to see you!"

Slowly, he turned his head and realized the woman racing toward them looked like an older version of Rose. Her hair was dark, with streaks of white around her face.

The man still standing on the platform didn't look happy. And dread started to creep in as Elijah realized he had to be looking at Rose's parents.

Another taller man stepped down from the car and looked around in disdain at the small town they'd stopped in. But as soon as his eyes found Rose, his face lit up. Elijah fought against the jealousy he could feel raging inside him as he noticed how well dressed and immaculate the man in front of him looked.

By now, the woman was hugging Rose and crying with how much she missed her. Rose had her arms around her, but she lifted her head to look at Elijah. He could see pain in her eyes as she carefully watched him.

"Rose Lambert. Do you want to tell me what you were thinking running off to the other side of the country without a word to any of us?" The man was stomping toward them, so Elijah instinctively moved to stand between them.

He put his hand out to the man. "Sir, my name is Elijah Thorpe. Welcome to Squirrel Ridge Junction."

The shorter man reluctantly put his hand into his, shaking it quickly. "I'm Andrew Lambert, solicitor at Lambert, Davis, and Harvey in Ottawa. I'm here to collect my daughter and take her back home."

Anger welled up inside Elijah at how the man had already dismissed him to move toward Rose, determined to drag her back home. The look on her face indicated to everyone watching that she wasn't happy to see this man.

"I'm not going home, Father."

Everyone around them went quiet as Rose stood firm. Her mother pulled back, and quickly brought a hanky to cover the sob that escaped as Rose spoke.

"Yes, you are. I don't know what you were trying to prove by taking off out here, but I won't have it. Did you think I wouldn't find you?" Her father shook with anger.

"No, I knew you'd find me. But I also knew by then it would be too late."

Elijah watched as the man's face turned an ugly shade of purple as he struggled to control his fury.

By now, the other man who'd stepped out of the car had come over and put his hand on Mr. Lambert's shoulder. "Andrew, let's just go somewhere more private so we can all sit down and talk about everything civilly."

Something about the man made Elijah nervous. He was a tall man with not a single hair out of place. He wore a suit that looked like it had recently been pressed, and that he hadn't just sat in a train car riding across the country.

He put his hand out to Elijah.

"Thanks for the welcome. My name's Robert Harvey, Rose's fiancé."

CHAPTER 14

*R*ose's eyes hadn't left Elijah's face and she wanted to move closer to him, grab him by the hand and get him away from the platform they stood on. Joel looked ready to come over and throw Robert to the ground, while Evelyn looked at her with concern.

But Elijah just stood staring at Robert, letting his hand drop as they finished shaking. Slowly, he turned to look at her. "I find that difficult to believe, since Rose is now my wife."

"Your *wife?*" Her father's voice roared in her ears.

She whipped around to face him.

"Yes, Father. *His wife.* Which I'm sure you already knew was going to happen since you managed to find me out here somehow." She was shaking with anger as she confronted her father.

"I knew you were planning to marry some Mountie out here in British Columbia, but the man I hired to find you didn't mention the marriage had already happened. I thought you'd have more common sense than to marry the first stranger you happened upon just to spite me."

"Andrew, dear, calm down. There's no sense making a scene." Her mother turned to her, and Rose wanted to shout at the woman to stand up to her husband for once. "Rose, why don't we all go back to your place, and you can show us to our rooms."

Rose clenched her teeth together as she fought her anger. "Mother, I don't have rooms. I have *a* room. One room. You will all have to stay at the small hotel set up by the stagecoach station."

Her mother looked horrified as she quickly glanced around the dusty town. It was far from the atmosphere they were used to.

Robert had remained quiet, but now was moving slowly toward her. "Rose, I know we may have argued, but to run off like this was very unseemly. Does your new husband know why you had to run away so abruptly?" He turned to face Elijah, and Rose was sure her heart stopped when she saw the look on her husband's face.

"Rose?" Elijah wasn't listening to Robert. He was giving her the chance to tell him herself.

"Robert and I were promised to be married, but it was never an engagement I agreed to." She tried to move to Elijah, but he backed up slightly.

"So, you had an argument with your fiancé and decided to get back at him by coming out here to marry a stranger?" His voice sounded hurt, and she just wished everyone else would leave so she could explain it all to him.

"No. He tried to ruin my reputation and force me to marry him, so I took matters into my own hands and decided to get away from him." She whirled around to face her father. "And away from people who never let me make my own decisions about my life. Who would have more concern about their own standing in society than to believe that the man they were forcing their daughter to marry accosted her to ensure she had no other choice."

Tears were falling down her cheeks as she looked around at the shocked faces staring at her. Once again, she was sure everyone had already made up their minds. Her new friends would think she was some kind of spoiled rich girl who was mad at her handsome fiancé.

But the one that stung the most was the way

Elijah was looking at her. He believed her parents and Robert. He thought the worst of her.

"I came here to find someone who could possibly care for me, and maybe have a chance at a normal life, away from the stares and the restrictions of the society life you expected me to live."

"Rose, you've always had anything you ever wanted. What do you have now? A one room shack that you live in, in the middle of a run-down town. You won't last a month."

Robert was looking at her in shock, shaking his head as though he just couldn't understand what she was saying.

"And I never forced myself on you, if that's what you're implying. You were quite happy to let me kiss you."

She balled her hands into fists and started to move closer to Robert. At this point she didn't care if her husband had to arrest her for beating up a man.

"All right, that's enough. I think everyone needs to get some rest and try to have this discussion in a more private location." Joel had stepped forward, and was now in the middle of them. He turned to face her parents, and Rose caught a glimpse of Evelyn standing to the side. Her friend offered her an encouraging smile, so she could only assume Evelyn had asked her husband to step in.

Rose quietly mouthed a thank-you to the other woman.

"I will escort you to the rooms in the hotel, while Elijah and Rose head home. Whether you believe it to be true or not, they are married, so whatever your concerns are, they will have to wait."

"I will not be sent away without a chance to speak to my daughter in private. Don't you know who I am?" Her father was fuming as he faced the two Mounties.

Finally, it was Elijah who spoke. "Unless your name is Sir Wilfrid Laurier, I don't care who you are. I have no obligation to do anything you ask, and I certainly do not take orders from you. Now, you can walk away on your own, or I can take you in to our office and detain you for being a public nuisance. I'm sure since you've pointed out exactly who you are back in Ottawa, you can understand how the law works."

By now, her mother was crying and they had managed to draw a large crowd that was gathered around them. Squirrel Ridge Junction didn't have a whole lot of excitement, so this was something no one wanted to miss.

Her father squinted his eyes together as he pointed his finger at her. "This isn't over, young lady. You might think you've won, but I can assure you, I will make sure this *marriage* of yours never happened."

He stormed away, and her mother and Robert followed, with Joel right behind them.

"Elijah, I can explain everything. I wanted to tell you what happened back home, but I was scared you wouldn't believe me."

He was looking over her shoulder, and she could see the muscles in his jaw moving as he fought his anger. She put her hand out to place on his arm, but he pulled it away.

"Rose, you should have trusted me. I don't know what to think right now."

He turned and walked back to his horse that had remained grazing next to the platform. Throwing his hat on his head, he hopped onto the horse and pulled on the reins to turn it around.

She stood with tears falling as she watched him ride out of town. With a sinking feeling in her stomach, she was sure he was also riding out of her life for good.

CHAPTER 15

*H*e couldn't get the look in her eyes out of his mind. Everything that happened on that station platform played over and over in his head, while he tried to get comfortable on the hard ground, looking up at the stars above him.

She'd been hurt as he'd walked away, but he'd been so angry he was scared of what he'd say.

Why hadn't she just told him the truth? He could tell after just meeting the man one time that Robert Harvey was a swine. And Elijah hated to say anything bad about anyone, but Rose's father was even worse. It was no wonder she'd had to run as far away as she could get.

But the fact that she hadn't trusted him enough to tell him the truth bothered him. He'd always tried to be a fair and patient man, and he thought Rose must have known that about him by now.

Suddenly, a loud noise cracked in the woods beside him. Jumping up, he grabbed his gun and pointed it in the direction the sound had come from. In the light of the full moon, the moose that was always hanging around town, ambled out of the bushes and stared directly at him.

Monty.

That was the name Rose had told him Miss Hazel had given the moose. It seemed like a fitting name for the big animal that was standing in front of him. He knew moose could be dangerous if provoked, even this one that the women had all decided should be some kind of pet.

Did he have something hanging on his antlers? From here, if he didn't know any better, Elijah was sure he was walking around with a pair of women's underthings draped over the top of his left antler. And on the right side was a shawl he'd seen Rose wear more than once.

Monty shook his head at Elijah as though even he was angry that he hadn't stayed to talk things over with Rose.

"Well, what do you know you big, blundering clod?"

Elijah ended up shaking his own head as he realized he was trying to rationalize with a wild animal. To be fair, though, Monty was hard to consider in a class of wild animal as he stood shaking the women's clothing free from his antlers.

"Fine. I will take these back to Rose and sit down and talk to her. Is that what you want?"

Deciding he was truly losing his mind, he realized he needed to get home to speak to Rose before he started imagining the animal talking back to him. Elijah walked closer to pick up the clothing that was now lying on the ground. Monty gave him a nod and turned to walk back into the bush he'd come out of.

Grumbling under his breath at the ridiculous animal that was always hanging around, Elijah folded his bedroll and threw his leg over his horse. He tucked the clothes inside his bag and headed for home.

No one would ever believe he'd just had Monty the Moose tell him he needed to get home to his wife.

He wasn't even sure he believed it himself.

ROSE LET the coolness of the approaching autumn

air kiss her cheeks as she sat on the front step. She could see every star for miles, and the light from the full moon was reflecting off the mountains in the distance. The sound of an owl calling out in the darkness of the woods outside of town sounded sad and lonely, mirroring her own feelings.

After Elijah had flown out of town on his horse, she'd walked back home alone, determined to make him listen when he got back, whether he liked it or not.

Only, he hadn't come home. She'd eaten dinner alone and sat waiting to hear the sound of him coming through the door. When she went to bed, he still wasn't back and her stomach was in knots as she worried what would happen.

Once again, her father had made sure she had no control over what happened. He'd purposely come here to destroy anything she'd done without his consent. He could never let her have any say, and if he thought she'd somehow "won," he wasn't going to let it go.

She felt terrible that Elijah had been dragged into all of it, but she'd gotten the impression from Miss Hazel that this Mountie she was coming to marry needed her just as much as she needed him.

Now she wasn't so sure. Everything was in a

mess, and she hated to think what everyone in town must be thinking of her.

A wealthy, spoiled harlot who had been caught with a man outside of marriage, and who had run off to teach them all a lesson after a silly argument. At least that was the picture that was being painted.

Tucking her feet up under her warm nightgown, and pulling her knees up so she could rest her chin on them, she wished she could pull her favorite shawl around herself for warmth. But thanks to Monty, she was sure that shawl was halfway across British Columbia.

The only company she'd had today after the scene at the train station had been the silly moose who stumbled through her wash line. He'd brought a smile to her tear-stained face, and she'd been sure he'd stood watching her for a long time before racing off into the bushes faster than she'd ever seen him move.

"You look a bit chilly. I thought you might like to have this."

Rose jumped at the sound of Elijah's voice. Her head flew up and she saw him standing at the edge of the step holding her shawl in his hand. He moved closer and laid it around her shoulders.

"Thank you. I thought for sure I'd never see it again."

He reached into his bag and pulled out the other item Monty had run off with. She was horrified as Elijah handed them to her with a sheepish grin.

"Oh, my…thank you."

He came over and sat on the step beside her, letting one leg stay straight out while the other one bent to rest his arm on. He was looking down at the ground, seeming to be interested in the dirt under his shoes.

"I never heard you ride back into town." Her voice sounded loud in the stillness of the night around them.

He nodded slightly and lifted his head to look up at the stars. "I came in the other way so you wouldn't have heard me. I just got back."

She knew he hadn't been assigned to go out on rounds, but she decided not to question where he'd been. If he'd needed some time to figure everything out, she was glad to give it to him.

They sat together, quietly listening to the lone howling of a wolf in the distance. The sound was eerie, making Rose shiver.

Suddenly, Elijah's arm came around her and pulled her in to his side. He still hadn't said a word, but somehow she felt safer. With a relieved sigh, she let her head fall to rest on his shoulder.

This man had every right to be angry, and even hate her for what had happened today. Yet here he was, letting her know he wasn't just going to walk away from her without giving her a chance to explain. He was willing to believe in her, which was more than any other person had ever done for her in her life.

As she sat beside him, soaking in his warmth, she realized that somewhere between needing to get away from home and finding her own life, she'd fallen in love with the Mountie she'd married.

CHAPTER 16

"Rose, you know your father means well, and he only wants what's best for you. You've broken his heart by running away like this."

She was sitting in the small dining room of the hotel across from her mother, while her father and Robert had gone to the telegraph office to send a message back to their firm. She was sure they were probably looking into what they could do to make sure her marriage wasn't legal, but she didn't care.

She was staying here with Elijah, and there was nothing they could do to stop her.

"Mother, the only thing Father has ever cared about is what will be beneficial to him and his career. He doesn't care what I do, as long as it suits him."

"And poor Robert. He was devastated when you

ran off. The humiliation he had to endure. You're lucky he's still determined to marry you and give you the security of his name."

Her mother wasn't even listening to her. She'd become so accustomed to listening to her father and blindly following everything he said, the woman couldn't even think for herself. She truly believed everything she was saying, even though anyone with eyes in their heads should have been able to see the truth.

"Lucky? Mother, he was the one who ruined my own good name, or have you forgotten that? He forced himself on me, knowing we would be caught. I'd told him our engagement was off, and I didn't care what Father said. So Robert made sure I was left with no choice but to marry him. And neither one of you cared about how that made me feel. You were all too worried about your own good names."

"Rose Lambert, that's not true."

"My name is Rose Thorpe now, Mother."

Her mother waved her hand dismissively as she shook her head. "That's no matter, dear. Your father will fix all of that, and before long we will all be headed home."

Rose could feel her anger rising, and she knew she had to try and keep it under control. There were other people in the dining room, and she didn't want to do anything that would embarrass Elijah in town.

Standing up, she pushed her chair back and stepped away from the table. "Mother, my home is here, in Squirrel Ridge Junction, or wherever else Elijah might get stationed. He's my husband, and I won't be going anywhere unless it's with him."

She spun to walk out of the room, without realizing the tablecloth had become caught on the clasp of her skirt's waistband. The entire setting on the table crashed to the floor amid the horrified stares of the other guests. Her mother's hand flew to cover her mouth in shock, while Rose closed her eyes and counted softly in her head. Maybe if she just pretended she was somewhere else, she could be whisked away without anyone seeing her.

When she opened her eyes again, she was mortified to see Elijah standing at the doorway, arms crossed in front of him as he shook his head slowly in her direction. "I don't know what it is you have against dishes, Rose, but I have to say you certainly know how to make an exit."

"You know, my father isn't likely to just leave

quietly without trying to make me go with him. He won't give up until he's won."

Elijah raised his arms and brought the axe down hard, easily splitting the big log in half. He'd been trying to build up the pile of wood for the winter, but since Rose had arrived, he'd been neglecting his work. Chopping wood was always the best way to get his anger out, so he figured today was a good day to get back at it.

He threw the split pieces to the pile and looked over at Rose. She sat on the back step watching him after she'd finished hanging the washing. He couldn't believe a girl who'd grown up with the life she'd had was able to adjust to doing menial tasks like laundry so quickly, but he was learning that Rose was a lot stronger than anyone had ever given her credit for.

"Well, do you want to go?" He found his stomach quickly knot up as he asked the question.

She brought her eyebrows together in a scowl. "Of course not. I meant what I said. I didn't just come out here because I was trying to get back at my father, or because I'd had an argument with Robert. I came here because I wanted a new start away from the life I'd had, with everyone telling me how to act, what to wear, even what to think." She put her head down and looked at her hands clasped together resting on her knees. "I came here hoping maybe I could find someone who would care about me, and not the money my family has."

Her last sentence came out so quiet he almost didn't hear her.

Feeling like a heel, he realized since her family had arrived a few days earlier, he'd been punishing her by blaming her for not telling him everything. Since meeting them all, he could understand why she hadn't.

And, he could see why she wanted to get away.

Setting the axe down, he wiped his forehead with the cloth he had sitting beside him and walked over to the step. "Rose, I'm not going to let your father drag you back to Ottawa. He can do whatever he wants to try and find a loophole that will say our marriage isn't legal, but he won't win this time. As much as I might not have believed I needed a wife, I've got to admit I've got used to having you around."

He cringed again as soon as he said the words. They weren't exactly the flowery, poetic words that told a woman he cared about her.

She brought her head up and laughed softly. "I'm glad, I guess. It's good to know someone has become used to having you around."

He crouched down in front of her and took her

hands in his. "That's not really what I meant. I mean I like having you here, with me. Sometimes I don't say things the way I want to. But, I do want you to stay here. Your father might think he can make you go home, but he will have to go through me to do it."

He thought he could see her eyes welling with wetness, but she quickly blinked and smiled at him. "Somehow I get the feeling my father might have met his match."

Bringing his hand up, he cupped her cheek, rubbing his thumb along her soft skin. She leaned into his hand and closed her eyes. Feeling his chest clench, he moved in and gently brought his lips to hers. As soon as they touched, a fire ignited inside and he knew he was losing himself to this woman.

Her hands went around his back, pulling him toward her, almost causing him to lose his balance. His hand moved into her hair, bringing her closer as his lips moved on hers.

When he finally pulled his head back, he looked down into her eyes and smiled. "And Rose, I can assure you, you've found someone who doesn't give a whit about your family's money. All I care about is sitting right here in my arms."

CHAPTER 17

"'d make sure you think long and hard about your decision. This kind of money could help care and provide for your grandmother for the rest of her life. She wouldn't want for anything."

Elijah clamped his teeth together tightly to keep from telling Andrew Lambert exactly what he thought of him and his "offer". The man had come in to the station this morning to speak to him alone, and had decided to offer Elijah more money than he could hope to make in ten years working as a Mountie. But the catch was, he'd have to release Rose from their marriage so she could return to Ottawa with them on Thursday.

Thankfully, that was now only a couple days away. The time they'd already been there had worn on Elijah, and he knew it had been difficult for Rose. After rescuing her from the restaurant and paying for another set of china, he had taken her home and they had talked, with both of them seeming determined to stay together.

Even though, Robert seemed intent on making her see what she'd missed out on, and her mother just cried every time she saw her.

Her father was a completely different story, and had spent the week wiring back to Ottawa and trying to figure out how to get Rose out of the marriage.

Now, the man had decided to take matters into his own hands, hoping Elijah would be swayed by the promise of money. While there was nothing he wouldn't do for his grandmother, he knew she'd never want any money given with these stipulations.

"Sir, with all due respect, I think you should understand that your daughter made a choice to come here and be married. It would be nice if you could respect her decision and be happy for her, but if you can't, I'm going to have to ask you to leave. I'm her husband now. So as far as anyone having the right to make any decisions for her, that's now on my shoulders." He leaned back in his chair and crossed his arms in front of him. "Although, as I'm sure you already know, Rose is more than capable of making her own decisions."

He kept his gaze on his father-in-law, making sure the man understood he couldn't be bought—for any amount of money.

"Rose was promised to Robert for a long time, and she hadn't complained once. Just because they had a falling out, it's no reason to throw away the history the two of them have together. Robert is heartbroken at losing the woman he loves, and I'm not happy that a promise I made to him was broken."

"A promise *you* made? What about Rose? Did she ever have any say in it?"

Elijah could see that Andrew was getting angrier by the redness filling his face. "Rose always knew what the plan was. Robert Harvey comes from a long line of big name solicitors in Ottawa, and to have him as a partner in my firm is a huge asset. Her duty was to marry him to ensure the bond of our families to work together."

It was times like this when Elijah was thankful for the simple upbringing he'd had. Even though they'd sometimes had to go without and times had been tough, at least he wasn't seen as a way to bring more wealth to his family.

Standing, he smiled to himself as the shorter man

stepped back so he could look up at him. He came out from behind the desk and reached out to grab his red coat from the hook by the door.

"Sir, I appreciate the fact that you've come all this way to ensure your daughter's well-being." He almost choked on the words, knowing how much of a lie they were. "However, I offer my word that she will be taken care of and will never want for anything."

Andrew Lambert laughed cynically. "What can you give her? Eventually she'll miss her life of being pampered, with maids and cooks to take care of her. Right now she might think she's having fun playing the happy wife on the frontier, but I promise you, I know my daughter. She won't be happy living out here, living in a shack, and relying on a Mountie's wage."

Elijah stopped halfway through putting his arm into his sleeve. He didn't want to give the man the satisfaction of seeing how much his words had affected him. He'd had his own worries about it since finding out Rose had come from a wealthy upbringing.

He kept his back to the man as he heard him shuffling toward the door.

"I'll let you think about my offer. Rose would

never need to know. Just hop on your horse and ride away until I can get her away from here. And you can become a very wealthy man."

The door slammed and Elijah was left standing in the silence of the room. He put his jacket on the rest of the way, and worked on doing up the buttons. He had to go out on patrol so he didn't have time to deal with Rose's father right now. In all his life, he'd never met a man so arrogant and inconsiderate of others.

Especially his own child.

He found himself feeling a tremendous amount of sadness for the life Rose must have endured while growing up. He was surprised that her kindness hadn't been tainted by the coldness of the man who'd raised her.

Although in all likelihood, Rose had probably spent most of her time with maids and other servants who would have provided what her own family couldn't.

His heart broke for the little girl she must have been, and he vowed he'd make sure the rest of her days were filled with all the love she could imagine.

Because no matter what her father offered him, Elijah was not letting Rose get away.

HE HATED BEING AWAY from Rose this long, especially knowing her father and ex-fiancé were there. He wished they'd just hop on the next train, which would be arriving today, and go back home. They'd been here a week and hadn't succeeded in finding anything wrong with their marriage, so hopefully they'd give up and be gone when he got back to town.

He'd left town immediately after talking to Rose's father in the Mountie's station, determined to get this set of patrols done quickly. He wanted to go home to let Rose know that no matter what had happened, he wanted to make theirs a true marriage, and that he'd somehow fallen in love with her. His problem was going to be finding the right words. He had to say what was in his heart without messing things up when they were spoken out loud.

But things hadn't gone smoothly, and he was already gone a day more than he should have been. He'd been on patrol alone this time, doing some routine checks in the area. So he was in a hurry now to get back to town, pushing his horse to go as fast as she could go. He didn't want to give Rose's father any more time alone with her than he had to.

As though the weather understood his mood, the skies seemed to open fully, bringing down a torrential rain. He pulled his heavy jacket tight around his neck and hunkered down in the saddle, watching the rain pour from the front of his hat onto the horse's neck.

Another hour and he would be home. He hoped the rain would let up before then, but by the color of the sky he didn't hold out much hope.

Suddenly, a loud crash of thunder and a flash of lightning hit a tree a few feet in front of him. His horse spooked, rearing up as one of the larger branches came down, hitting him hard in the chest. Falling back off the horse, he tried to get his hand out to take some of the impact.

As his head hit something hard, he had a vision pass by of a beautiful woman with the blackest hair smiling down at him. He tried to reach for her, but she was fading from his view.

When blackness overtook him, his last thought was that he hoped she wouldn't go back with her father.

CHAPTER 18

"We aren't going home and leaving you here alone."

Rose took a deep breath and tried to smile. "Father, I'm not alone. I have Elijah, and I have my friends I've made. If you don't get on this train, you'll be stuck here for another week until the next one comes through. Is that what you want? I know your stay here hasn't lived up to the standards you are used to."

The Pullman car had been disconnected when they'd arrived and left at the station in Squirrel Ridge Junction for the Lambert's to use for the trip back to Ottawa. It still hadn't been hooked back to the train that had just pulled in, because her father was still insisting he wasn't leaving without her.

Robert was pouring on his charm, knowing Elijah had been on patrol for the past couple of days.

"Listen, I didn't want to have to tell you like this. But since you've said yourself that Elijah isn't normally gone this long, I think it's best I tell you the truth."

Dread pooled in her stomach as she looked at her father and waited for him to continue.

"I decided to test your husband just before he left on patrol. I offered him a good sum of money that he could use to look after his grandmother…"

"Father! How could you? How do you even know about his grandmother?" Rose was horrified at what Elijah must have been thinking.

"Do you think I'm not going to investigate and find out everything about the man who married my daughter? I know he has a grandmother who still lives on her own, struggling to get by. And I'd say by the fact he's been gone longer than he should be, he's decided to take me up on my offer."

"What are you saying, Father?" She spoke through clenched teeth.

"I told him if he wanted the money, in return for letting you out of this marriage, to ride out of town until I could take you home."

She swallowed the doubt that threatened to rear

its head. The Elijah she'd gotten to know over the past three weeks didn't care about money like that, did he? But she knew he cared about his grandmother. He'd never left any question about that.

Would he have wanted the money to help the woman he loved above anyone else? Rose couldn't really blame him if he did. His grandmother had raised him and given him everything she could.

But her heart still stung at the thought.

Lifting her chin, she turned to walk away. Her parents and Robert were free to stay, but she wasn't standing here listening to them anymore. She just wanted to get home, away from the eyes of everyone who were sure Elijah had chosen the money over her.

"Rose, there's someone here I think you should meet." Theodore met up with her, pulling an older woman along with him, her arm tucked neatly into his.

She put on a smile, even though she was sure everyone could tell her heart was breaking.

"This is Pearl Thorpe, Elijah's grandmother."

Rose's mouth opened in shock as she tried to figure out what to say. "You're his grandmother? Oh my goodness, Mrs. Thorpe, I had no idea you were coming! Elijah hasn't mentioned it at all. I'm so sorry! I would have met you here if I'd known."

The small woman laughed and reached out to take her hand, patting it between her own. "That's because I didn't tell him I was coming. I wanted to surprise him, much like he did with his letter to me announcing he was married."

"He'll be so upset that he wasn't here to greet you. He's on patrol, and has been gone a couple of days now." Rose's mind was racing as she tried to figure out what to do. She wanted to get Elijah's grandmother back to their house before her parents or Robert came over to continue their conversation.

"So, you're Elijah's grandmother? It's so nice to meet you. I'm Rose's father, Andrew Lambert. I'm sure you were just as shocked to hear about their marriage as we were."

Too late. Of course her father would have heard everything. She was surprised his investigator hadn't already informed him that Mrs. Thorpe was on her way out to British Columbia.

The kind woman shook her father's hand with a smile. "It was a shock, but now that I've met your daughter, I can see why he'd be smitten so easily." Mrs. Thorpe was still holding on to her hand and squeezing it as she looked at Rose.

"If you ladies want to come with me, I'll get your bags, Mrs. Thorpe, and escort you both back to Elijah and Rose's place."

Rose sent Theodore a grateful smile, knowing he was aware of the situation with her parents. She could see he was doing what he could to help her get away without incident.

Elijah's grandmother let Theodore take her hand once more, tapping him gently on his shoulder as she shook her head. "I wish you all would just call me Pearl. You make me feel like an old woman calling me Mrs. Thorpe."

Rose grinned at Theodore who was now staring at Pearl in shock. He was quite obviously unsure how to respond. But it didn't matter as the older woman started walking over to the bags lying by the side of the platform, practically dragging Theodore along behind her.

As Rose started to follow, someone grabbed her arm. Whirling around to see who had stopped her, she shook her head at Robert.

"I would suggest you get your hands off me, Robert. Theodore isn't far away, and I'm sure a Mountie would be obligated by law to enforce punishment on anyone mishandling another officer's wife." She used to be intimidated by this man, and the power he had over everyone around them.

But she wasn't anymore.

"You're making a mistake, Rose. I won't wait forever. Now that your Mountie has taken off, waiting for you to go back to Ottawa so he can collect his money, you aren't going to be left with many other options. I'd suggest you think about what you're doing before you push me away again."

Yanking her arm from his grasp, she turned to see Elijah's grandmother watching them closely. She put on a smile, hoping the woman wouldn't see how upset she was.

Rose walked over and hooked her arm in the other woman's and they followed Theodore back home. As they made their way along the street, Rose couldn't stop wondering where Elijah was. He should have been here to greet his grandmother.

She tried to ignore the ache in her heart as they made their way home. Feeling the woman beside her give her hand a tight squeeze, she turned her head and met bright blue eyes that reminded her of Elijah's.

"Whatever is worrying your pretty head, my dear, you can just let it go. I know my Elijah, and I can tell by the words he wrote me that you've become important to him. He might not have been able to let you know himself, but I know what's in my grandson's heart."

How could Pearl have known what she was thinking?

She didn't know, but she realized that this woman walking beside her knew Elijah better than anyone. She would trust her to be right.

The alternative was just too painful to believe.

CHAPTER 19

Elijah tried to move, but every time he went to sit up, his head would spin. He knew he had to get to his horse, and hope she could carry him back to town. The rain had finally let up, but he was wet and cold. He also knew he still had a ways to go before he got back to town.

He pushed onto his elbow to try once more. Pain shot through his ribs, forcing him to lie back down. He clenched his eyes tight to try blocking the pain.

He knew he was at the mercy of any wild animals in the area, as well as the elements that were leaving him vulnerable. He could already feel his body shivering from the wetness, and as the night grew colder, he knew he was going to have to fight to stay warm. If only he could drag himself somewhere that would provide some shelter.

As the hours went by, he drifted in and out of consciousness as he struggled to keep warm. The warm trickle of blood coming from the back of his head dripped down his collar.

This was exactly why he hadn't wanted to get married. How would Rose manage on her own out here?

He cringed as he realized she'd be left to deal with her father, who would most likely drag her back to Ottawa to marry that pompous man who'd tried to ruin her reputation.

No, he couldn't leave her like this. He'd drag himself back to town with his bare hands if he had to.

He started to pull himself up, hoping the pain would eventually ease. But he couldn't get anywhere without seeing stars and feeling like he was being ripped in half. He fell back against the hard ground, cursing to himself at his own stupidity. He should have been paying more attention to the road, and riding to the conditions.

Instead, his mind had been on Rose and how he needed to get home to see her.

Hearing a noise in the bush, he reached down to see if he could grip his gun. As he did, pain shot through his ribs again, and he knew he'd never have the strength to pull it out. Just as blackness overtook him again, he made out the faint outline of familiar antlers making their way out of the trees.

"Look after her for me, Monty. Don't let them make her go back."

His words were mumbled as he let the darkness win.

~

"DEAR, you're going to leave a hole in that mat if you don't sit down." Pearl had brought some knitting with her and she was sitting in the rocking chair next to the window, busily clicking her needles together.

"Mrs. Thorpe, why don't you get some sleep? You must be exhausted after your trip here." Rose turned and smiled at the woman. It had been dark for a few hours already, yet the woman refused to go to bed knowing how worried Rose was about Elijah.

Rose had set the bed up for the woman to use and had planned to lay some extra blankets on the floor for herself, even though the woman had insisted that she could share the bed with her.

Rose couldn't figure out what it was that was bothering her, but something just didn't feel right.

Even though her father had tried to make her believe Elijah had run, wanting to get the money from her family, Rose couldn't believe it.

But as the hours ticked by, she had more doubts creep in. When Theodore had asked her if Elijah had come home yet, she'd noticed the flicker of worry in his eyes too. He'd said it wasn't usually a patrol that would take this long, but perhaps Elijah had run into something that was holding him up.

She'd seen the concern in the other man's face.

"I've already told you to just call me Pearl. Or, you can call me Grandma, since we are family now." The woman winked at her as she continued to knit without even looking at what she was doing.

Rose moved to sit on the other chair by the table. "I've never had a grandma. Well, I did, but I never knew them. I always imagined having a grandma would be wonderful."

Pearl set her knitting on her lap and looked at her with a puzzled expression. "You poor child. Everyone should have a grandma."

Rose shrugged and laughed softly. "I always thought so too."

They sat quietly for a while, listening to the sound of the wood in the stove that was keeping the house warm from the chill of the night.

"You know, I was sure surprised when Elijah sent me a letter saying he'd got married. I had no idea he was looking for a wife. He'd always said he was going to stay single so that he didn't have to worry about leaving a wife behind, like his pa had done to his own mother."

"He told me his mother died of a broken heart." Rose watched as Pearl nodded her head sadly.

"When my Pete died, poor Alanna was sick with grief. But she'd contracted pneumonia shortly after my boy was shot, which was what really took her, even though Elijah always believed it was her broken heart."

"How awful for him, to be left without any parents." Rose imagined the young boy, with his curl hanging down in his eyes, grieving for both parents at the same time. She was glad he'd had his grandmother to care for him.

At least he'd had that much.

"It's nice of your parents to have come all this way to celebrate your marriage."

Pearl was watching Rose closely, making her statement almost sound like a question. Rose was quickly finding out that Elijah's grandma was a very perceptive woman.

But she didn't want to burden her with the details of her own situation.

"Yes, they arrived over a week ago."

Pearl continued watching her, until Rose was sure she'd have to pour out her entire story to the woman.

"You love Elijah, don't you?"

Rose's eyes suddenly filled with tears. What was wrong with her? The woman had simply asked a question, and she was ready to break down in front of her.

Nodding her head, she wiped at her eyes and stood up, bringing her hands down to smooth out her skirt.

"It's complicated. We were married without really knowing each other. And I wasn't really sure I could fit in and manage here. The poor man hasn't had a decent meal since I arrived, because I can't cook. And truthfully, I'm sure he wishes I'd just hop on the first train out of here so he didn't have to worry about having his house burned down to the ground when I try to make him a simple meal…"

"Rose! I can assure you, Elijah doesn't think any such thing."

Swallowing the lump in her throat, Rose moved over to look out the window into the darkness. She'd let all the worries tumble out and now she probably sounded like a fool. Thankfully, tonight Jess had brought some extra food over that she'd made to welcome Pearl to town. So, she hadn't had the misfortune to see how bad things really were for her grandson.

As she stared out toward the trees at the edge of town, she saw something move out of the corner of her eye. Probably just Monty up to no good again, she thought to herself.

Her heart jumped into her throat though as she realized it was Theodore and Kendall, racing toward her house. Another horse was running behind, without a rider.

Elijah's horse!

Where was he?

She stumbled to the door and threw it open, racing out onto the step as the men pulled up outside.

"Rose, we found him lying on the ground about an hour outside of town. He's bleeding pretty bad from his head, and he hasn't regained consciousness at all since we got him."

She ran toward Theodore's horse, finally noticing the figure slumped over in front of him. She reached up to try and help, but was quickly pushed back by

Kendall, who had already dismounted and rushed over to help Theodore get Elijah to the ground.

A sob escaped from her throat and she brought her hands up to cover her mouth as she saw the blood. The men carried him into the house and straight into the bedroom, while she ran ahead to pull the sheets back on the bed.

Lifting her head as the men placed Elijah on the bed, her eyes met Pearl's and she could feel the anguish in her own heart as they both silently prayed for him to be all right.

CHAPTER 20

She wrung the cloth out and placed it back on his forehead like she'd done since the others had left hours ago. Light was starting to come in between the opening in the curtains, yet she still hadn't seen Elijah open his eyes once.

Theodore and Kendall had wrapped his head with some cloths to stop the bleeding, but they said they couldn't be sure how hard he'd hit it. They also didn't know how long he'd been lying out there in the cold, wearing his wet clothes.

They'd mentioned some worries about pneumonia and other conditions she didn't understand, because her mind had been so consumed with worry.

She stood and pushed on the ache in her back. She needed to stretch her muscles after sitting on the edge of the bed all night. She wasn't surprised to see Pearl sitting in the chair knitting as she went into the other room. Since she hadn't been able to use the bed, Rose had tried to lay out enough blankets to make a soft enough bed for her to sleep on, but she could tell the woman hadn't slept at all.

"Good morning, Rose. I've made us some coffee."

She smiled at Pearl. "Thank you. I could use a cup."

"How's he doing?"

Rose could see the hope in his grandmother's eyes. "He's still resting, so that's good." She honestly had no idea how he was. He hadn't woken up since the men brought him in, and that scared her.

But she didn't want to let on and cause Pearl to worry too.

Hearing a knock at the door, she walked over to answer it. Theodore stood there with another man she didn't recognize.

"I've brought Doc Sturgis over to take a look at Elijah. He'll check to see if he has any other injuries, and make sure he's not getting any infection or anything else to worry about."

She opened the door wider to let the men in. "Thank you, Theodore. He still hasn't woken up, and

I've been keeping cool cloths on his head like you asked me to."

She showed the Doc into Elijah's room, then went back to sit with Pearl in the other room. Theodore followed her out and sat down at the chair across the table from her.

"Elijah's tough, and just stubborn enough that I know he'll pull through. So, try not to worry too much, Rose. He's going to need you to take care of him until he's feeling better."

She nodded and smiled at Theodore. She appreciated that he was trying to ease her worry.

"How did you know where to find him? I didn't get to ask you anything last night during all of the confusion and chaos of bringing him home."

"Well, after dropping you both off at home, and you mentioning he still hadn't come back, I couldn't shake the worry that something might be wrong. So Kendall and I decided to follow the roads he'd have taken for his patrol." Theodore stopped and shook his head slowly and gave a short laugh.

"We might have ridden right past where he was lying in the dark if not for a strange snorting noise that drew our attention. There was Monty, standing off to the side, as though he was guarding Elijah on the ground. As soon as he saw us, he turned and ran back into the woods."

Rose could picture it, and she had to smile. Somehow she wasn't surprised in the least that Monty would be around somewhere during it all.

Suddenly, a loud wail could be heard coming from the bedroom. Theodore jumped up and raced in to help the doctor. Rose followed, stopping in her tracks at the sight of Elijah moaning in agony as the doctor wrapped some tight bandages around his chest.

"Looks like he might have a broken rib or two. Not much we can do for that except try not to let him move too much."

Rose stepped around the doctor and sat on the edge of the bed, taking Elijah's hand in hers. She looked down into his face, noticing how red it had become since she'd left him.

"Is he awake?" She turned to look at the doctor in confusion.

"No, he was just responding to the pain of being moved." The doctor closed his bag and stood up to leave. "Just keep him comfortable, and hopefully time will help to heal his injuries. Not much else we can do except pray at this point."

She didn't even turn as the men left the

room, reaching back into the bucket of cold water she'd left in there to soak the cloth again. She wrung it out, listening to the droplets hitting the water in the pail. Placing it on his head, she struggled to keep her tears from falling.

He looked so fragile lying there with his curl hanging down over his forehead and his eyes clenched closed. She pulled at the blanket to bring it up and cover his bare chest above the bandage. Never in her life had she felt so helpless.

Feeling a hand on her shoulder, she raised her head to see Pearl staring down at the man on the bed. Seeing the love in her eyes tore at Rose's heart. She could never imagine having anyone love her the way this woman did her grandson.

If love could heal Elijah, Rose knew that there was more than enough in this room to save him.

THE OTHER WOMEN had taken turns bringing food over for them, and sitting with Rose, while Pearl took turns with Elijah. At night, Pearl would sleep at Jess's, and Rose would curl up in a chair next to his bed.

He still hadn't woken up, and every day that passed scared her even more.

As she sat staring down into the face she'd come to love, she leaned over to place her head gently on his chest, careful not to hurt his ribs. Hearing his heartbeat and feeling his chest rise and fall with each breath was a comfort, knowing he was still with her.

Pearl had already left for Jess's for the night, so Rose was left with only the sounds of his rhythmic breathing to break the silence in the house. She'd been sleeping on this chair for the past couple days now, and exhaustion had taken over.

As she faded into sleep, she dreamed that Elijah was awake. She could feel his fingers caressing the skin on her cheek, and moving into her hair to brush it back. Sighing, she let herself enjoy the feeling of him being back with her.

"Rose, as much as I could lie here and look at your beautiful face all night, you're hurting my ribs."

The chest beneath her rumbled, and with a start, she realized she'd fallen asleep but she wasn't dreaming. She whipped her head up, and as she tried to stand, she fell forward, narrowly missing elbowing Elijah in the ribs.

"You're awake!"

His face was grimacing as he tried to smile at her.

"I am. I didn't want to disturb you, but the pain was becoming unbearable."

"Oh, I should go get Theodore or maybe Doc Sturgis. Just stay there…are you hungry? I can get you something to eat. No, let me get you a drink. The only fluids you've had the past few days are the bits I've been able to get down your throat while you slept."

She turned to run to the door so she could get some fresh, cold water from the pump.

When she came back in, she rushed over and tried to help him sit up. Lifting the cup to his mouth, his eyes closed as he savored the wetness of it touching his lips.

After he'd finished, she set the cup down on the table by the bed and stood up. "I'll go get Theodore now."

She didn't know what else to do. Her heart was telling her to throw herself on him, telling him how much she loved him and was thankful he was alive. But she also wasn't sure how he'd react. These feelings were all so new to her, and he'd just been through a serious injury. She knew with her track record, she was likely to break a few more of his ribs if she tried anything like that.

Before she could get away from the bed though,

Elijah reached out with his hand and grabbed hers. "No, just stay here with me. You look like you haven't slept in days. The only thing I need right now is you beside me."

"But…" What did he mean?

"Rose, just this once, could you do something without arguing with me? I've got lots of room beside me, and nothing would make me feel better than having you here with me."

"What if I hurt you?" She'd thought of just crawling onto the bed beside him many times over the past few days, but had been afraid she'd bump him or do something that would cause him even more pain.

"You won't. Just come and lie down so you can get some sleep. We'll let everyone know I'm okay in the morning. For now, let it just be us."

His voice still sounded raw from days without speaking, and she could see he was in some pain as he winced when he moved slightly. But he still held her hand and wasn't letting go.

"Just lie with me."

As she looked into his eyes, she knew there was nowhere else in the world she'd want to be. Moving around to the other side of the bed, she gently crawled on top of the blankets, careful not to bump him. He put his hand out for her, and she slowly tucked herself into his side.

The sound of his breathing soon told her he was asleep again. But this time, she didn't have to worry that he wouldn't wake up.

Letting herself drift off to sleep, she knew that in this moment, this man had become her whole world. And she would never let anyone take him from her.

CHAPTER 21

"*I*'m fine. I'd be a lot better if you two women would stop fussing over me. I'm a grown man, and I think I know if I can stand up on my own or not."

He was sitting on the edge of the bed trying to stop the room from spinning, and both Rose and his grandma were hovering and fretting that he should stay in the bed.

"Just wait until Theodore gets here. What if you fall?"

He took a deep breath and sighed.

"Rose, just come here and let me put my arm around your shoulder to steady myself." He couldn't lie in this bed another minute. He was humiliated at having his needs tended to by his wife, grandmother and his friends. He was sure if he got up and moving around, he'd be fine.

"Well if you end up falling and breaking anything else, you have no one to blame but yourself." Rose came over and leaned down beside him, helping him get his arm around her shoulders.

She stood, helping him to stand. He couldn't believe how weak he felt, but he wasn't going to let these women know that. They'd be insisting he get back into the bed.

He'd been so surprised to see his grandmother when she came to the house in the morning. She'd promptly scolded him for scaring her so badly, then hugged him until he'd thought he would pass out from the pain.

Seeing his wife and grandmother together, he realized how much they had in common. Well, except that his grandma was the best cook in the world, but he was sure in time Rose might be able to improve in that area.

They were both strong women, who had a kindness that sometimes people mistook for weakness. And they were both fiercely protective of him at the moment.

They slowly made their way to the other room, and just when he thought he would make it to the rocking chair without incident, Rose bumped into the side of the stove, jerking her hip into him. They stumbled slightly, and he had to reach out to grab the side of the counter to stop himself from falling.

Wincing in pain, he sharply took a breath in, hissing through his teeth.

"Oh, Elijah, I'm so sorry! I told you this wasn't a good idea."

He stood for a moment with his eyes closed, waiting for the pain in his ribs to subside a bit.

How could he tell her that he'd expected at least one incident to happen before they made it to the chair? He loved this woman, but she had a tendency to be less than graceful most of the time. Although he had to admit to finding it somewhat endearing most of the time, right now he wasn't appreciating it as much.

"It's fine. Maybe we should walk out more toward the middle of the room where there's less chance of you running into anything."

He was almost sure he saw her eyes flash with a hint of anger at his insinuation, but she quickly hid it as they started to walk again. He smiled to himself knowing how much she likely was biting her tongue to not say anything to him at the moment.

When he was sitting in the chair, she went to get

back up but he held onto her hand so she couldn't stand. Staring into the big, dark eyes looking back at him, he smiled. "Thank you for getting me here in one piece."

"Next time you might not be so lucky." She gave him the biggest, sweetest smile she could, letting him know she didn't appreciate his attempt at humor.

Walking away, she turned to his grandmother. "Now that he's up, I'm going to run to the store to get some of the supplies we need." She looked back at him and tilted her head slightly. "I hope you won't grumble too much for your grandmother."

He leaned back and grinned. He knew maybe he hadn't been the best patient, but he was sure he wasn't as bad as she made it out to be.

"I promise to be on my best behavior, until you get back."

He waited until she caught what he'd said, then grinned as she shook her head and walked out the door.

Knowing how easy Rose was to rile up, he realized he was going to thoroughly enjoy spending his life with this woman.

~

SHE WALKED OUTSIDE, holding her basket that she'd filled with everything they needed. Pearl had been showing her some of her favorite recipes, especially ones she'd said Elijah loved.

Tonight, she was going to show her how to make his favorite stew, so Rose had grabbed all the ingredients they would need.

It was a beautiful day, with a hint of a breeze blowing through the trees around the town. She smiled and said hello to the residents who approached her asking about Elijah. She never would have dreamed living in a small town like Squirrel Ridge Junction could make her feel so happy.

Seeing her father and Robert walk toward her from the hotel across the street, she took a deep breath and waited to speak to them. She'd almost been able to forget that they were still here—and had told them firmly that while she was caring for her sick husband, she didn't have time to visit with them. But she wished she could have spent some more time with her mother, although since she seemed unable to see how wrong they were being in trying to force her to go back home, Rose had avoided her too.

"Hello, Father. Robert"

She knew he probably wasn't marching over to her to make small talk, so she braced herself for whatever he planned to say to her.

"Rose, I've been patient long enough. You're coming home with us on that train tomorrow."

Sighing loudly, she shook her head. "I don't know how many times I need to tell you—I'm not going home with you. This is my home now."

He shoved a paper in her hands. "You might want to read this. I'm certain your Mountie husband wouldn't like to have something like this leaked to the world. That's if he even knows himself. Can you imagine how he would feel to find this out?"

She noticed Robert standing with a smug smile on his face, which sent a chill down her spine. Scared to read what was on the page in front of her, she slowly put her eyes down to the paper.

As she read, her stomach knotted and her hands started to shake.

Raising her eyes to meet her father's she struggled to see him through the wetness blurring her vision. "You just can't give up until you get your way, can you?

"I expect you to be at the train station when that train arrives in the morning. I'm sure your Mountie will be more than happy to let you out of your marriage after you've run back home." He turned to walk away. "And if you decide not to show up, you can be sure that everyone will find out the truth that you're holding in your hand."

Crumpling the paper into her fist, she watched them leave. Robert grinned back at her, sure he was finally going to succeed in having her.

She had no other choice. She couldn't let Elijah find out the truth. And if it got out to the world, his reputation and that of his family would be ruined.

CHAPTER 22

Sleep wouldn't come, and as she lay next to Elijah listening to his even breathing, her heart ached knowing how hurt he was going to be. He'd never come out and said it, but she'd started to believe he might care for her.

And as much as she wanted to tell him how she felt, she knew it wouldn't be fair now. Slowly crawling out from her side of the bed, she tiptoed to the other room. She let her eyes look around, letting herself see everything she'd come to love about this place.

It was nothing compared to what she'd had growing up, but the memories she'd already made in this small cabin were much happier than any she'd had in her large house back in Ottawa.

This place felt more like home than anywhere she'd ever known.

Swallowing hard, she moved over to the door, opening it and to walk out onto the front step. She didn't want to wake Elijah, and she knew her nervous pacing inside would be too loud. Hugging her arms in front of her, she looked up at the stars in the sky. The mountains stretched as far as she could see, and it seemed like the peaks were reaching up to touch the moon.

Suddenly, someone grabbed her arm, pulling her to them while covering her mouth so she couldn't scream. Not that she thought Elijah would be much help at the moment, but one of the other Mounties might have heard her.

She was dragged across the road and into the bushes on the other side, as she tried to kick and hit at whoever it was who had her.

"Stop it, Rose. It's just me."

Robert!

"If I take my hand away, you have to promise not to scream."

She glared at him in the darkness, not even sure if he could see her face. So, she tried to bite his hand to let him know how she felt about being dragged into the bushes.

"Ouch!" He pulled his hand back and shook it.

"What are you doing? It's not enough that you've already managed to destroy my husband's name if I don't go home with you, so you decide you need to kidnap me too?" She was shaking with rage.

"Well, Rose, I know you enough to know you'll likely try to pull something to get out of coming home with me. So I decided to make sure your husband wouldn't want a woman who'd sneak off into the bushes with her old boyfriend. A soiled woman isn't a good choice for a Mountie."

Her heart raced as she looked around for an escape. She could scream now, but she knew she was too far for anyone to hear her. Robert was strong, and he was holding her arms tight in front of her.

"I've missed you, Rose. I can't wait to start our lives together." He brought his head down and tried to kiss her, but she turned her head.

Pushing her to the ground, he hissed, "You've always thought you were better than me. You didn't know how good you had it, to be marrying Robert Harvey. Do you know how humiliating it was for me to hear that you ran off to marry someone else?"

As he started to crawl on top of her, she tried to bring her knee up, but he pushed it down with his hands.

Suddenly, she heard loud snorting coming from the bushes beside them.

"What was that?" Robert quickly turned his head, distracted for a moment. She pushed at him and managed to throw him off. He reached out and grabbed her arm as she tried to get away.

But before he could pull her back down, Monty ambled out from the bush, snorting directly into Robert's face. She almost laughed out loud at the terror she could see in the man's eyes.

Monty didn't move, standing nose to nose with him as Robert slowly stood up. The giant moose stomped his front foot on the ground, and that was all Robert needed to turn and run. He raced out of the bushes, never even looking back to see if Rose was all right.

She backed away, remembering Elijah saying just because he might be cute, Monty could still be dangerous. As she looked at him now, though, she didn't believe it. If she could, she would have hugged the animal for being her savior.

However, before she could even contemplate the safety of that idea, Monty looked at her, then turned and went back into the bushes.

She decided she wasn't going to stand there and wait to see if Robert would return. Although the last she'd seen of him, he was flying up the street toward the hotel with his feet barely touching the ground.

Running back to her house, she got inside and closed the door quietly behind her. She only had a few hours to decide what she was going to do, so she moved to sit in the chair to calm her nerves while she came up with her plan.

She just hoped Elijah could forgive her someday.

CHAPTER 23

*H*e stretched, wincing slightly still as the pain from his ribs reminded him of his injuries. He had to admit he enjoyed waking up with his wife beside him, feeling the softness of the fabric of her long nightgown keeping her covered as she snuggled up beside him.

But something was different this morning, and his eyes whipped open as he realized she wasn't beside him.

He was surprised he hadn't felt her get up. He slowly set his legs over the edge of the bed, sitting there for a moment until his head stopped spinning. He was still struggling to move as quickly as he'd like, but at least he could manage on his own a bit now.

Rose must be out trying to make him breakfast.

He could hear the sound of pots scraping on the stove, and the smell of coffee reached his nose. She'd come a long way since arriving, and at least now he was able to swallow most of the food she made.

When he walked into the other room, he saw his grandmother standing at the stove, with no sign of Rose anywhere.

"Elijah, here, come sit down at the table." His grandma raced over as fast as her short legs would take her to pull the chair out for him.

"Thanks, Grandma. Where's Rose gone off to already this morning?"

His grandma patted his hand, and clucked her tongue like she always did when she was trying to soothe him. "Oh, I'm sure she'll be back in no time."

But something in the way she said it didn't seem right to him. "Grandma, you didn't tell me where she went?"

She was back at the stove, stirring the eggs she'd cracked into the pan.

Why was she avoiding his question?

"Grandma?" He slowly stood up from the chair and walked over to her, taking her shoulders and making her face him.

"Elijah, I don't want you worrying. I've gotten to

know Rose very well since I came to town, and I know she'll do the right thing. She'll be back."

"What's going on, Grandma? Either you tell me, or I'm going to head out that door and find out myself."

His poor grandmother scowled at him, then moved past him to the chair she sat in to do her knitting. Bending down to reach into her knitting bag, she pulled out a crumpled piece of paper that was singed around the edges.

"I found this caught in the lid of the oven when I went to stoke the fire this morning. It's a telegram addressed to Rose's father."

Elijah read the words with dread. He should have known Andrew Lambert would keep digging until he found something he thought could hurt him.

"But what does this have to do with Rose? Even if she read it, why would she care so much?"

His grandma patted his hand. "Well, I suspect her father is trying to make her go back with them on the train that will be arriving today. I found this note on the table this morning."

She reached into the pocket of her apron and pulled out a small piece of paper. He recognized Rose's handwriting.

Dear Elijah,

I'm so sorry for the pain my family has caused. I hope someday you can forgive me.

Love always,

Rose

His heart stopped beating as soon as he heard the whistle of the approaching train. His eyes turned to his grandma's and she gave him a sad smile.

Rose was just going to leave, like that, without even saying goodbye? He'd honestly started to believe she cared about him. How could she think that anything her father could do would ever matter to him?

He wasn't letting her go—not like this.

Spinning as fast as his wounded body would let him, he ran outside. Every breath he took felt like his chest was on fire, but he moved as fast as he could toward the train station at the end of the street.

He knew he didn't have much time. The train didn't sit long in Squirrel Ridge Junction before moving on to the next town on its stop. *Why wouldn't his legs move faster?*

He could hear voices arguing at the station as he came around the corner, and the conductor yelling about a moose standing on the tracks.

Somehow, Elijah just knew it was Monty.

~

"GET THIS TRAIN MOVING. Just hit the moose if you have to. I'm not waiting another minute."

Her father's voice rang out as he yelled from his special car that had been hooked back up to the train for the ride home. Rose stood near the open door of the Pullman car, ready to tell her family her decision.

Everyone had already assumed she was going home since she'd shown up and was standing in the car. But what they didn't know was that she was getting off the car as soon as the train started to move.

She wasn't going home with them. However, she also knew the only way to get them to go was to pretend she was.

"Rose!"

Her heart jumped into her throat as she heard Elijah's voice. She turned and looked out, seeing him struggling to run and get to the train. She tried to step out, but her father grabbed her by the arm, holding her.

"Get this blasted thing moving now!" He yelled at the conductor from the doorway.

But thanks to Monty, the train wasn't moving anywhere.

Pulling her arm from her father's grip, she jumped down to the platform and ran to Elijah.

"What are you doing here? You're in no shape to be running outside like this!"

He looked at her incredulously.

"I find out my wife is about to hop on a train and ride back to Ottawa, and you think I'm just going to sit down next to my grandmother knitting in her rocking chair and spend the day chatting?"

She pulled her eyebrows together and shook her head. "Elijah, I wasn't going anywhere. I was coming to say goodbye to my parents."

"No you're not, young lady. You know what will happen if you're not on this train." Her father had stepped down behind her.

Elijah looked over her head at her father. "Sir, I've tried to be patient with you while you did everything you could to make Rose go back home with you. But you've gone too far this time. Rose is a grown woman who can make her own decisions, and nothing you say or do can change any of that."

"Elijah, he found out some stuff about your father." Rose didn't want to have to tell him, but he deserved to know the truth.

He looked down at her and smiled. "Like what? That he accidentally killed an innocent man during the shoot-out he was in? And when he thought that's what he'd done, there was speculation he'd taken his own life?"

He already knew everything.

"Rose, something your father neglected to mention to you was that while my father did kill a innocent man who'd gotten caught in the cross-fire, the truth came out that he hadn't taken his own life. Yes, he'd been shot with his own gun, but he hadn't pulled the trigger. And, even if he had, it doesn't change anything. Keeping all of that secret from the world wouldn't matter if it meant I lost you."

He brought his hand up and gently touched her cheek.

"Nothing matters except how I feel about you. You've somehow managed to charge in and crash into my world. I'm not good at saying how I feel, but I know I love you, Rose. And if you get on that train, you may as well take a knife and stab me in the heart."

She reached up and put her hands on his shoulders, blinking against the tears that were falling.

"I love you too, Elijah. I would never have got on

that train. You have my whole heart, and leaving you isn't something I could ever do."

He wrinkled his brows as he watched her in confusion. "But, you said you were sorry and you hoped I could forgive you someday."

She gave a little laugh. "I meant because I planned to tell my father I didn't care what he found out about you or your family, I wasn't going to let you go. I was being selfish because I knew I couldn't leave, even if it meant having your father's good name smeared."

Elijah's smile spread across his face as he brought his head down to hers. Pulling her close, he whispered, "Nothing in the world would matter if I didn't have you."

His lips touched hers, and as she kissed him with all the passion in her heart, the train's whistle shrilled.

They could hear her father cursing as her mother called for him to get back on the train. As he muttered and climbed onto the train that was getting ready to go, he made sure to leave her with some parting words.

"You haven't won young lady. You'll come crawling back, I know you will."

He had no idea how wrong he was.

Elijah pulled back and smiled at her. "Looks like Monty has moved off the tracks."

Pulling his head back down to hers, she silently thanked the silly moose that had always seemed to be right where he was needed.

She remembered Miss Hazel saying something to her long ago about the moose knowing where he belonged, and that someday, Rose would know too.

As she stood in Elijah's arms, listening to the train pull away, she finally understood what the woman had been saying.

Right here, in this man's arms, was the only place she belonged.

*R*ose smiled down at the baby in her arms, still in awe at the miracle she'd just created. Lifting her eyes to Elijah's, she shook her head in disbelief. "Can you believe she's so perfect?"

He grinned as he kept his eyes on his new daughter. "I can believe it. She's just like her mama."

Laughing, she shook her head at him. "I'm far from perfect, and you know it."

Shrugging, he took the baby from her arms and cradled her into his chest. "You're close. Even if you *have* managed to do some damage along the way."

He winked at her as she huffed in indignation. "Why do you need to bring that up now?"

He pretended to be shocked as his eyes met hers.

"Bring what up? I was merely saying you were close to perfect, however a bit on the dangerous side too."

She crossed her arms in front of her and pretended to be angry. In truth, she couldn't really be mad because she knew what he said was the truth.

As she looked around the bedroom that had been constructed on the new house, she figured at least everything had been finished in time for the baby to arrive.

Shortly after Elijah's grandmother had gone home to pack her things to move back out to British Columbia to be closer to her family, Rose had been trying to make one of the dishes Pearl had shown her.

Elijah had come home and distracted her, causing her to forget what she was cooking, so in truth she wasn't all to blame for the fact she'd managed to burn their house down around them.

Luckily, no one had been hurt and they'd managed to get the fire out quickly.

But they'd been left with a pile of rubble, so the other Mounties and townsfolk had gotten together to build them a new one. And this house, had room to expand as their family grew.

It even had a room for Pearl, who'd managed to arrive back in Squirrel Ridge Junction just in time for the birth of her great-grandchild.

"So, what do you think of the name Claire?" She looked back at the man who stood staring down at his daughter with a face full of love.

"I think it's a beautiful name."

"Claire was my best friend back home, and I'd like to name her after her. She was the only one I really had to confide in while I was there."

She thought back to her friend who'd been so excited for her to come out and meet "her Mountie". She'd written to her to tell her how right she'd been about everything.

Her parents had gone back to Ottawa, with Robert in tow. She'd never mentioned what Robert had done that night to Elijah, because she knew he'd be livid. The only one who knew was Monty, and she was sure he'd never tell. If Elijah had found out, she knew he'd want to make the man pay, but Rose just wanted them out of their lives for good.

She'd also written to her mother a few times, and was surprised when her mother had written to say how happy she was for Rose to have found a man to love her.

While she wished she could have had a better

relationship with her parents, she knew it would now be her turn to make sure her own children had the kind of childhood she'd longed for.

Squirrel Ridge Junction had become her home, and the people in this room were her family. She laughed as the door opened, letting in the rest of her "family."

Pearl led the way, with the other Mounties and all their wives and some new babies behind them. These people had given her more love than she could have ever hoped for, and she knew she would never trade it for the world.

Turning her head slightly, she shook her head and laughed again at the sight out her window.

And of course, how could she forget Monty, who was once again tangled in the clothesline out back.

The moose lifted his head and looked in the window, then gave it a shake and walked away, leaving a trail of destruction behind him.

Elijah came over and sat beside her, while Pearl took the baby from his arms. Everyone followed her to get a good look, so he leaned down and whispered in her ear, "I love you, Rose."

Smiling up at him, she reached up to push the curl off his forehead.

"Even if I'm not perfect, and managed to burn your house down?"

He grinned at her. "You make my life exciting. What more could a man want?"

Pulling his lips to hers, she closed her eyes and let him show her. And she knew without a doubt, this Mountie had her whole heart.

∾

*I HOPE **that you enjoyed RNWMP: Bride for Elijah!***

If you could take a couple minutes and head back to Amazon to leave a review, it would be truly appreciated :)

***FOLLOW the Mail Order Mounties Amazon author page and join the Private Facebook Readers Group just for fans of the series!**

MAIL ORDER MOUNTIES

*Join our Facebook Readers Group - https://www.facebook.com/groups/MailOrder-Mounties/

*FOLLOW our Amazon Author Page - https://www.amazon.com/Mail-Order-Mounties/e/B071KJ3B17

ABOUT THE AUTHOR

Kay P. Dawson is a mom of two girls, who always dreamed of being a writer. After a breast cancer diagnosis in 2011, she decided it was time to follow her dream.

Years of reading historical romance, combined with her love for all history related to the old west and pioneer times, she knew that writing in the western historical genre was her calling.

She writes sweet romance, believing a good love story doesn't need to give all of the juicy details - a true love story shows so much more.

**I have a Facebook fan group set up for anyone who enjoys my books, and reading in the sweet western romance genre - and I would love to have you join us! There are special giveaways and fun events just for members...and a place just to hang out with others :)

You can join at: https://www.facebook.com/groups/kaypdawsonfans/

**Newsletter SignUp:

http://www.kaypdawson.com/newsletter

OR TEXT 'DAWSON' to 42828

Made in the USA
Middletown, DE
26 December 2017